"I love the prophetic and I love to see how it can be demonstrated through many forms and manifestations. Gail Hamlin does a wonderful job with her new book, *"Prophetic Utterances – The Cry of His Heart"* Volume One. She shows the heart of the Father to us using poetry. These poems reflect God's heart and feelings for people, letting them know that ultimately God has a good plan for their lives and a good future for them to look forward to. This book has been a long time in the making, but now, its time has come. I recommend this book. No matter what you are facing, you will find a word for you straight from the heart of God. The words that God speaks are truly sharper than any two-edged sword. You will be encouraged. You will be lifted up. You will know you are loved."

Mary Dorian
Assistant Pastor
Glorybound Ministries Center

"I met Gail Hamlin approximately 10 years ago in church. In those 10 years, there is one thing that has not changed in her- her love for our Lord Jesus Christ. Secondly, she is an avid writer who has not stopped writing and is always thanking God for giving her the words.

She served in a Women's Jail Ministry team with me, where she ministered the word and shared some of her writings with the women. They found comfort and encouragement in her words. As we all go through rough patches in our personal lives, she too was not spared. However, with God, she has overcome health and personal issues time after time. She has raised four children who love God. We continue to keep in touch and she has been more excited than ever about putting together her writings with the goal of having a book published. I have no doubt that this will come about soon with much success." *"Delight thyself also in the Lord, and He shall give thee the desires of thine heart."* Psalm 37:4

Maria Barela
Coordinator, Women's Jail Ministry
Church Alive

The Cry of His Heart

Volume One

Gail Hamlin

Prophetic Utterances: The Cry of His Heart, Volume One
Copyright © 2018 by Gail Hamlin
Life Poured Out Publications

This book and parts thereof may not be reproduced in any form, stored in a retrieval system, or transmitted in any form by any means—electronic, mechanical, photocopy, recording, or otherwise—without prior written permission of the publisher, except as provided by United States of America copyright law.

Unless otherwise noted, all Scripture is taken from the New King James Version®. Copyright © 1982 by Thomas Nelson. Used by permission. All rights reserved.

Artwork by Lynn Bacharka (lynnmarie.co)

ISBN: 978-0-9974202-2-7

Library of Congress Control Number: 2017948423

Printed in U.S.A

This book is dedicated to:

My Love,
The LORD, my GOD who has
loved me
for better and for worse
in sickness and in health.
You have never left me or
fallen out of love with me.
You are the Husband that stayed
and happily provided for me.
You never treated me like
a burden.
Thank You for believing in me
when I didn't believe
in myself.
Your great love
washes over me
again and again.

I not only dedicate this book
to You,
but also my life and my love.
I dedicated all my children
to You and You have
been faithful in
raising them up to
be amazing people.
I thank you so much
for that.
You have been faithful,
merciful and gracious

Prophetic Utterances

to me,
and I am so grateful.
Thank You for using
me as Your pen.
It has been my
great pleasure
and honor to
serve You.

ACKNOWLEDGMENTS

To my children, Rachel, Jacob, Alicia and Aaron, and their spouses, the loves of my life: thank you for your love and support of my book. I appreciate all the ways you helped me fulfill this dream and desire to publish these writings. May God continue to bless you and all the works of your hands, for His glory.

To Kathy, my best friend and sister in the Lord: you stood by me through thick and thin in all ways. You supported me during this whole writing and publishing process, and you have encouraged me again and again to keep going. When I would get discouraged and put the writings aside, you would pull them out and ask to read them again, because you said they ministered to you when you were down and they gave you hope when all your hope was gone. You helped me believe the words were relevant to others and should be shared, and I thank you for believing that the writings were indeed inspired by God, Jesus and the Holy Spirit. Thank you for believing in the God in me. Thank you also, for your input and editing help all along the way.

My gratitude goes to both Kathy and her husband David Schaffer who have supported me in so many ways: too many to count. They have been friends and family to me, and I love and appreciate them so much. Thank you for supporting me in all my endeavors. May God richly bless you as you have blessed me.

To my pastors at Glorybound Ministries, Claudia Baca-Moore, Wyatt Moore, and Mary Dorian: your transparent and genuine love for the Lord touches my heart deeply. You always seek the presence of the Lord, both in worship and in your sermons. I am sure this pleases the heart of God. Thank you for your support of this project and for your belief that it is God who qualifies a person. I appreciate how you encourage people to reach their God given destinies. You pack a powerful punch throughout the world with God's mighty hand and prophetic voice.

Prophetic Utterances

To Michael and Selina Lombardo and their publishing team: thank you for taking on this publishing endeavor and working with me. Thank you for your help and support throughout this project. May God richly bless everything you do.

To those who have helped me financially with this project: I thank you from the bottom of my heart for your belief and support, and I will be forever grateful.

CONTENTS

FOREWORD	13
INTRODUCTION	15

PART ONE
Writings from 2002

THE HARVEST OF THE LORD	21
THE FEAST OF FOOLS	26
THE GOD OF THE UNIVERSE	27
AMIDST THE PERILS GREAT	30
I HAVE CALLED YOU	31
HE IS THE MASTERPIECE OF LIFE	33
WHEN THE HEAVENLY CONNECT	35
THE MAKER OF THE CLAY	37
HE HAS DRAWN YOU	38
THE DAY OF DELIVERY	39
THE GREAT MAGISTRATE OF ALL	41
THE DESIGNER FROM ON HIGH	45
THE GOD	47
MY GOD	49
THE DESIGNER OF MAN	52
THE GOD OF ALL MIGHT	57
YOU ARE MY DESIRE	59
THE DAY OF DOUBLE PORTION	61
THE CHURCH IS UNDER ATTACK	62
THE SECRETS OF THE BOOK	64
I AM THE AUTHOR	66
THE GREAT HIGH GOD	68

YOU'VE BEEN COMMISSIONED	73
THE PRINCE OF THE HIGHWAY	75
THE GODFATHER CLOCK	77
THE SELF-MADE MAN	79

PART TWO
Writings from 2012-2014

THE GLORY OF GOD	83
THE MESSAGE OF THE CROSS	92
THE WALLS OF INJUSTICE	94
A BRAND NEW DAY	95
HE IS GOD	99
THE GREAT GARDENER	100
THE ENEMIES OF GOD	102
THE END DRAWS NEAR	104
THE MAJESTIC WARRIOR	110
THE FATHER OF HEAVEN	119
FOLLOW HIS LEAD	126
HIS ACT OF LOVE TOWARD US	128
I HAVE ORDAINED YOU	134
HE HAS ISSUED A CHARGE	136
HIS PLAN	138
THE DEMISE OF SATAN	142
MY SECOND COMING	147
THE DAY OF PREPARATION	151
THE DAY OF THE LORD	153
IT'S TIME FOR YOU	155
PREPARE FOR THE WEDDING	160
SATAN'S DEMISE	163
HOLD ON	171
THE DAY OF DOOM AND DREAD	176
THE DAWN OF THE MILLENIUM	183
HE LOVES WITHOUT END	184
WHAT LIES AHEAD	187
THE KING OF THE HEAVENS	193

I WAS UNAWARE OF HIS PRESENCE	196
THE KING OF WONDER	199
YOU LOVE US SO MUCH	201
YOU ARE THE KING ETERNAL	205
OUR GOD ETERNAL	208
THE HOST OF HOSTS	211
HEED MY WARNING CRY	215
IT'S THE ELEVENTH HOUR	220
THE ARTIST	224
THE MAD HATTER	227
DRIVING INTO THE SUN	231
THE KING OF THE UNIVERSE	233
THE FINAL JEOPARDY	235
THERE'S BEEN A CHANGE IN TIME	237
DON'T TOUCH THAT DIAL	238
WRITING ALL THESE RHYMES	239
THE DRONE OF DECEPTION	250
YOU'LL BE FREE	263

FOREWORD

As Pastors for 25 years, we have seen many types of writings expressing the voice of God. Some years ago, I wrote an entire book, start to finish, in one sitting. I felt God's presence so strongly and clearly as I typed the book. This experience tells me that God indeed can speak to a person, and they can capture it on paper. That's how the Bible was written—by man, but under the inspiration of the Holy Spirit. Its books and letters were written to certain groups of people, yet each one speaks to all mankind.

God still is alive and speaking in the same way. In *"Prophetic Utterances, The Cry of His Heart"*, Volume One, Gail Hamlin shares words, which she perceives, are from God—and they are. This book will speak to the hearts of many people. It will answer questions that may have arisen in the readers' hearts and minds, and it will also give inspiration to their souls.

Gail has a unique ability to bring out the prophetic voice of God in a delightful way. This book is very different than any that I've seen in the past. The writing will not only make God's voice sound familiar, its literary style is very artistic and creative. It is not a typical, *"Thus saith the Lord"* prophetic work. Instead, the writing is crafted in a very personal and poetic way that makes it easy to read, understand, and take to heart.

It is very obvious that Gail has spent much time in the presence of God, and that she has been trained in hearing His voice with accuracy. Gail brings out the beautiful colors of the living, ever present God.

Wyatt Moore and Claudia Baca-Moore
Pastors, Glorybound Ministries Center
Albuquerque, NM USA

INTRODUCTION

In 2002 (Part One) I said to the Lord, "God, don't you have anything new I could write about? The apostles of old never took Writing 101 and David just tended sheep; yet, You used all of them to write for You. I want to write a book inspired by You. Can you give me something? Don't you have something new? If I compare myself to the writers of the world, I won't want to write. I don't want to read all the things written by the best writers. I don't want their ideas. I want Yours. Please give me something." Then I heard the Lord say, "As it is written."

I thought, what? I heard it again, "As it is written." I thought, written? I hate my writing. I'm left-handed and in my opinion, I have ugly handwriting. I begged, "How about I type it on the computer?" I sat down like a spoiled child and put my hands to the keyboard. There were no words or thoughts in my head… then I heard it again, "As it is written."

My dad used to say, "There is more than one way to skin a cat." So I had another idea, I put some old disks into my computer to see what was on them and as I did this, my computer froze. It crashed. I promptly looked up and saluted Him and said, "Yes, Sir, as it is written!"

I marched upstairs, prepared an area in my bedroom with a nice armchair and table beside it. I lit a candle and sat down with a pen and notebook in hand and I said, "Ok, give it to me." I looked up at the ceiling and then at my notebook and anxiously waited and waited. I received nothing, so I called it a night.

The next evening, I repeated the same steps—I waited, waited and walked away again. So, on the third day I decided if it didn't work that night, I was giving up. I was feeling pretty stupid anyway and embarrassed, even though I didn't tell anyone what I was doing. The last night finally arrived. I waited and waited, but ended up giving up in despair and going to bed.

At about midnight, I was awakened from a sound sleep with all kinds of words pouring through my mind. I grabbed my pen and notebook and began writing quickly trying to keep up with them. They had a rhythm as they came. I did not hear a voice, only words. This went on for three days and three nights and it didn't stop. I had to jump out of the shower, soaking wet, and write what I was getting in there and then go back in and finish up. There were times I was driving and had to pull over to the side of the road and write. It went on and on and on. I filled up three notebooks and then as quickly as it started, it stopped.

Unfortunately, what followed was a complete crumbling of my life and family, as I experienced a severe reaction to a medication, which left me with devastating results physically. I lost my memory, mind and coordination. In the emergency room as I was being examined one doctor said to another, "Look, her eyes are fixed." I could hear them, but I couldn't respond. I wondered why the light didn't hurt my eyes as he was shining it in them. I asked God, "Where am I? Am I dead? Am I in a coma?" Luckily, that part didn't last too long, but it took me a couple of years to recover fully. It felt like my brain was constantly re-booting; I blinked a lot as I tried to talk and remember things. I lost function of my left-hand, my writing hand. I couldn't type or move my fingers well. I pushed myself to make them work again.

During my recovery time, I met an elderly Messianic Jewish man and I told him how my life had fallen apart. He read me Ecclesiasticus 2, out of the Apocrypha. "The fear of God in time of ordeal." It read: "My child, if you aspire to serve the Lord, prepare yourself for an ordeal. Be sincere of heart, be steadfast, and do not be alarmed when disaster comes, cling to him and do not leave him, so that you may be honored at the end of your days. And in the uncertainties of your humble state, be patient, since gold is tested in the fire, and the chosen in the furnace of humiliation..." That passage resonated within me because of my life experiences.

I then had a divine appointment with The Lord at Glorybound Ministries where guest speaker Michael Kristy gave me a prophetic word:

"Oh, there's something on you. I saw the glory of God being released to you. I just felt the gift of faith come on me in this building right now, and I saw the open heavens come to you. I saw the Father visit you. I saw you had a gift to write. I saw God giving you the ability to write, Psalms 29. Ascribe to the Lord, and the Lord's going to cause you to scribe to Him, ascribe to the Lord. It's a Psalm 29 anointing on your life. Release it, in Jesus' Name. Thank You, Holy Ghost, for the wells and the waves of the Father. There's a gift on her life to heal actual physical relationships between sons and daughters and the Father. That's what the Holy Spirit told me. You have a gift to help heal mom and dad relationships, and God's given you wisdom on that. Lord, release it in Jesus' Name; it's a counseling gift out of Isaiah 11, the spirit of counsel and might. Lord, I thank You for that in Jesus' Name."

About a month and a half later the next set of writings came to me (Part Two 2012-14) around the same time of year the others did. I hadn't prayed for more writings after that last episode, so I was surprised when God gave me more, especially after 11 years had passed. The rhythm was the same and the messages were similar in nature. It was a continuation of what He had spoken before, only this time they lasted about five weeks and then others trickled in after that.

From the time I received the writings until now, I have dealt with health issues including having multiple surgeries; bouts of depression, a degenerative disk disease in my neck with bone spurs, arthritis and two herniated discs. I have to have procedures done regularly to control the pain. I had an antibiotic resistant infection in my nose that almost killed me. Writing and health issues have been an integral part of my life, but by the grace of God I am still standing and pursuing God. The Lord spoke to me several times, on my darkest nights, "Not for a moment will I leave you!" He will see me through clear to the other side, whenever that time comes. Until then, I am hanging on tight to Him and the Word of God!

These writings are more than mere poetry—I feel that they are from the Lord's heart and include declarations, decrees, proclamations, warnings and pleadings. He has issued a charge, a declaration of war and has released a battle cry. I heard Him speak mysteries and tell me of the glory that awaits us. Through these writings He shares His immense love for us. He tells us what He loves and what He hates.

I used all caps for His names to show honor and reverence to Him. I also used caps when He repeated a certain word or theme. Also, He spoke words I had never used and I would have to look them up to see what they meant. If the word wasn't in the dictionary, I tried my best to sound it out and I put it in. I figured since God created words, if He wanted me to use one in a way I didn't understand, who am I to change it. He has poetic license. People are making new words all the time for technology, etc. I believe God can do as He pleases. I just wrote what I heard Him say.

Sometimes His voice was pleading, warning, and almost begging. Sometimes it was God speaking, other times it was Jesus, and other times it was the Holy Spirit. They are all One—they all serve a specific purpose. I sensed the urgency throughout the writings. I tried to stay true to His voice of urgency. This was not just a simple poem about a blade of grass or a leaf. This was ALMIGHTY GOD—THE GOD OF THE UNIVERSE. To me, He deserves the highest reverence we can give as humans. I felt compelled to express that emotion with the use of capitalization, italics, etc., to honor Him.

It is my prayer that you will feel the cry of His heart for you, His children. He loves you so much, and He is such a devoted Father. He knows we are tired and weary, but He wants us to overcome every obstacle. So, hold on, don't let go, get discouraged and give up. We win in the end. God is with us no matter how it looks in the world around us. There were too many writings to fit into one volume so Volume Two is in the works.

> *Jesus answered them, "I told you, and you do not believe. The works that I do in My Father's name, they bear witness of Me. [26] But you do not believe, because you are not of My sheep, as I said to you. [27] My sheep hear My voice, and I know them, and they follow Me. [28] And I give them eternal life, and they shall never perish; neither shall anyone snatch them out of My hand."*
> John 10:25-28

*"...For the testimony of Jesus
is the spirit of prophecy."*
Revelation 19:10

Prophetic Utterances

PART ONE

Writings from 2002

*"Call to Me, and I will answer you,
and show you great and mighty
things, which you do not know"*
Jeremiah 33:3

THE HARVEST OF THE LORD

Has come, ensuing fruit
already won!
It's time to move for it won't last
seize the fruit before it's past.

Send for the laborers
from near and far
before the fruit is spoiled
and THE HARVEST is lost!

Hurry! Come quickly!
Get into your place!
THE HARVEST is happening
all over the place.
The fruit is ripe,
it's easy to see,
and they're waiting
to be nudged off
from the tree.

How ripe is ripe you ask ME?
GOD ask THE FATHER
and then THE SON.
HE will whisper, *Get Going!*
Because, at last,
some ripen before others
and their richness
won't last.

THE HARVEST is coming.
Look into THE SON.
The fruit is popping up
all over the place
and the time has come
to save
the human race.

Prophetic Utterances

Send for the laborers
to pick really fast.
Remember... THE HARVEST
won't last!

Pick them quickly!
Handle them with care.
There really isn't
much space
left in there.
The baskets are loaded
*Don't leave them
in there!*
They will bruise
and turn brown
because they are so
far down.

The time for decision
is straight ahead.
Will you enjoy
some for now
and savor the stead?

THE MASTER has spoken
to your head.
What form will you give them?
Will you bake them or try
to turn them into sauce?
Could you make them
into a pie?
Will you seek to preserve them?
Come what may!

THE HARVEST is upon us
we must give them away!
Some will be savored
some will be chewed
some will be
purchased with a

The Cry of His Heart

coin or two.
Some will be waiting
while they are
beginning to bake.

THE HARVEST is upon us.
What form will they take?
Will they be changed into pastries
for THE MASTER to taste?
Will HE savor the beauty
and marvel at the taste?
And glory at the change in
HIS whole human race?
THE GOD OF THE HEAVENS
THE GOD OF US ALL

Is sending a message to all:

THE HARVEST
*is coming upon us
at last!!
Quick! Be Ready!*
The fruit won't last.
Seize the moment
So they don't chaff.

HE will never desert you,
you're the
apple of HIS eye.
HE *just* wants
to save you
before you shall die.
The ripeness will only last
but a time.
Eternity is forever,
and forever is long.

*Stand Up!
Get ready to pick!*
Ignore your tired flesh

Prophetic Utterances

until the last has
been picked.

Quick! Preserve them really fast!
Before THE HARVEST is done.
The fruit won't last.
The Jubilee is about
ready to start!
The Day has been beckoning
from within HIS heart.

*"Come meet THE MASTER,
you laborers"*
HE will say,

*"Come meet THE MASTER,
THE MAKER of the clay."*

HE is *thrilled* that
the treasure is so vast.
HIS *delight* is to
savor HIS splendid design.

HE is
THE GREAT GARDENER
from on high.
HE is
THE TREE OF LIFE.
Can't you see?

HE has created with purpose
and plans all about
preparing for the victory
in the world throughout.

HE *died* and *rose again*
to prepare the way
for this day!

The Cry of His Heart

HE is
our TREE OF LIFE
our representative stay.

Proverbs 11:30, Matthew 9:36-38

Prophetic Utterances

THE FEAST OF FOOLS

Some of them say,
"Of what is this peculiar day?"
Is the feast for fools?
Or are fools for the feast?

Come to the table.
THE MASTER
you must meet!

Are jewels for fools?
For surely, they are not!
They are holy and sanctified
for the throne up on top.

They will shine with brightness,
you'll see!
They will shine for
the whole world
to see.

These *jewels* are special,
so rare and divine.
Their emblems of love
that resembles a stud.

A sacrifice of their love
HE placed with precision
from heaven
in a manner divine
for the whole world
to gaze and look upon,
while they begin to dine.

Proverbs 31:10-31, Isaiah 61:10

The Cry of His Heart

THE GOD OF THE UNIVERSE

THE GOD OF THE HEAVENS
THE LORD OF THE EARTH
Has requested your attendance to:

The Show of all shows!
With the elect in your presence,
and asked you to dine
and watch how
HE turns
water into wine!

Watch as
THE MASTER
of the heavens entertains
by turning water into wine.
Look! HE is doing it again!

See *the wonder.*
See *HIS glory.*
The Show's about to start.
HE is THE REWARDER
of the chosen
who all did their part.

THE KING OF KINGS
LORD OF HOSTS
MAKER OF ALL THINGS

Come to witness
such a splendid thing
as the
angelic hosts of Heaven
are invited to sing.

They'll sing of HIS grandeur,
and HIS excellent design.

Prophetic Utterances

The reason you've been
invited to dine.

Gaze upon HIS magnificence
and welcome THE DIVINE.

THE LORD OF THE HEAVENS
THE HOST of all hosts
is getting ready
to prepare a toast.

HE will say, *"Halleluiah!*
For *The Glory* has come.
Come join in the feast
with
THE FATHER and THE SON."

HE will bless and congratulate
those whose talents HE did employ,
for assisting every
man, woman,
every girl and boy.

HE will say, *"Halleluiah!*
A job well done!"
THE CREATOR OF THE UNIVERSE
has just begun.

A Message from:

THE FATHER
THE MAKER of the clay
THE POTTER
is pleased to applaud
you on this holy day.

You'll have life eternal
and this is just the start
given to the *chosen ones*
who are the pure in heart.

The Cry of His Heart

He'll sing *Halleluiah*,
on this *New Day*,
and thank you
for answering so quickly
HIS call.

HE will sing
Halleluiah
to one and to all!
Tis the season for glad tidings
for The Show
is about to start,
Bless you all! Bless you all!
There will be no more night
THE KING OF KINGS, THE LORD OF LIGHTS
THE MAKER OF ALL THINGS
delights.
HE wants your presence
above all things,
and the sacrifice of the things
that eternity brings.

Luke 14:13-24, Revelation 19:13-16

Prophetic Utterances

AMIDST THE PERILS GREAT

With the chosen
on this date
for every sailor
who climbs aboard.

For everyone
who's willing to set sail
on toward the skies,
to seek out their
MASTER of the Seven Seas.

Reach into the heavens
to behold HIS eyes
and on our knees
will HE give us
the *keys*
that open up
The Mysteries
for all to see.

Now, reach
for the heavens
and the deep blue seas
and discover the treasures
that lie within and
join the fellowship with
THE CAPTAIN of the seas.

Isaiah 45:3, Matthew 13:11

The Cry of His Heart

I HAVE CALLED YOU

Do you hear the ringing?
The sounding of *the call?*
Is your volume set in place
to hear
the human race?

You better run!
The call won't wait
once the sound has begun.
Pick it up!
Hurry, fast!
The caller cannot stall
any longer.

Yes, at last!
The call was answered!
The ringing stopped.
The connection made
and not delayed.

Thus begins
your crown inlaid
with precious voices
through right choices.

THE GOD of all
allowed the call.
HE made a way
for the sake of the call,
and for the sake of us all.

THE GOD of choices
who desires
our *voices.*
Which one will HE choose?

Prophetic Utterances

Who will be
our provider?

Then GOD said,
I AM not dead! Nor
merely words running round
your head!

For I have bled
to save your soul
from
The Coming Dread
of a future untold.

I have bled to save
the dead.
I have not bled to leave
you with no one to wed.

For as it was in *The Old*
and now is written
in *The New,*
to save MY chosen few.
Every man and woman,
every girl and boy
at the altar of
the resurrected dead.

Psalms 145:17-21, Ephesians 1:17-23

The Cry of His Heart

HE IS THE MASTERPIECE OF LIFE

Come one, come all
for the sake of the call.
I will do something new
for every man, woman
and Jew.

I will draw a new piece.
You'll be with ME
from the start,
if you enter in
and do your part.
Don't depart!

The Show
is about to start.
HE will reveal HIS delight
as THE ARTIST shines tonight!

Hang on tight!
It's going to be a delight!
For THE MASTERPIECE has come.

See the source
from which all beauty
has come.

HE has no boundary
nor does it have a limit.
It's going to be the
world's best ever exhibit!

You're going to get to meet
THE FATHER and THE SON.
Discover the source from
which all beauty has begun.

Prophetic Utterances

It's bound to be a thrill!
You surely can't sit still!
It's sure to be so fun!

Come and bring your vessel
and get your fill.
For THE MASTER has delivered
and the best is yet to come.

Psalm 27:4; Isaiah 28:5

The Cry of His Heart

WHEN THE HEAVENLY CONNECT

It is such a time.
I recognize them
all the time.
There's brightness to their eyes,
a sparkle from the well
it flows over everywhere.

I'm drawn to them
we magnetize each other!
There is no way to deny it!
The immense love for one another.

We see it.
We embrace the oneness
of having found our own.
What a gift in the moment.
A gift in a stranger,
now a forever friend.

It is our divine appointment.
We divinely sought without knowing.
We picked each other up,
encouraged one another,
in a brief moment of the day,
as we traveled with OUR MAKER.

In HIS eternal unit of measure,
HIS clock sounds to heartbeats.
Time is kept standard by the need.
The alarm sounds when
a needy heart is at hand.

THE FATHER'S hands are outstretched
directing in the direction of eternity.
HIS outstretched arms never cease.

Prophetic Utterances

HE IS
THE OMEGA
OF THE TIMELESS
THE ALPHA OF THE TIME AT HAND

HE IS
THE GREAT HIGH GOD
OF ETERNAL TIME.
THE DESTINY is there,
you can hear HIS ticking,
if you're truly listening.

You can hear the sounding
of HIS heart within
your body pounding.

You can sense
the *urgency time* at hand.
The moment will pass
without a watchman at hand.

You'll miss the time,
if you are not connected to
THE GREAT FATHER of the timeless.
The eternal time is at hand,
from HIS hands to ours,
from our hands to HIS,
as we stretch forth
to the beating need of the time.

What time is it? You say,
It's time to hear
the heartbeat of
the eternal time at hand.

James 4:8; Revelation 22:13-14

The Cry of His Heart

THE MAKER OF THE CLAY

Is the maven of the vine.
THE RULER of divine.
Sent from above to instruct
and help us deduct,
while HE conducts
The Masterpiece of our lives.

HE is the *Only One,*
THE FATHER and THE SON
since the world began.

THE ONE from whence,
The Book began.
THE FATHER OF THE SON,
HIS glory is being revealed,
for all the world to see.

HE is *The biggest of big deals!*
THE DESIGNER of the wheel
HE is THE GLORIOUS ONE
THE MAKER OF THE SUN.

HE is THE GLORIOUS ONE
THE FATHER and THE SON
now and since the world began.
HE is about to put on an exhibit!

To reveal HIS one true love,
it won't be in the shape of a dove
since that has already
been fulfilled thereof.

John 3:35-36, Hebrews 12:2

Prophetic Utterances

HE HAS DRAWN YOU

With a line so fine
surely sublime
drawing you to the divine.

Look at your spine
and a day and time.

The Godfather Clock
is about to dock.

Will you open up the
harbor of your heart?

And relish in and savor
and not forget your neighbor
before THE SON sets sail?

Remember that we need
the head before the tail.

Soon, we will all hail
THE FATHER of creation.

The Voyage has begun!
Come and join *The Journey*
of THE FATHER and THE SON.

Matthew 22:36-40, John 10:30

The Cry of His Heart

THE DAY OF DELIVERY

THE KING desires to take HIS place
for the love of humanity,
the human race.

HE is there at the ringside.
The Battle has begun,
with the source from where
all pain and sorrow have come.

HE will make HIS last stand
since the world began,
as the wheel of life goes
round and round.
The Battle has been won!

HE will meddle with HIS medal
so the world will see.
With HIS arms raised
HE is in search
of you and me
as HE takes HIS place
in Zion.

Every person who
has breath will sing
and praise.

THE KING OF KINGS
THE GOD OF ALL
THE GREAT HIGH GOD
THE RULER and MAKER
of everything.

THE KING OF KINGS
will rise with ease

Prophetic Utterances

to take HIS place as
THE SAVIOR of our race.

For the love of one
the love for all
as the number one KING
and THE LORD of all and
THE GREAT HIGH PRIEST
THE GLORY OF GLORIES
as HE finishes HIS Story
to show forth HIS glory
from here to there and
everywhere.

THE SON OF GOD,
THE GREAT I AM
has sealed HIS Heavens
and secured the gate.

HE is wonderful!
HE is marvelous!
Our KING OF KINGS
THE LORD is great!
It is finished!!

Jeremiah 51:19, Revelation 19:11-16

The Cry of His Heart

THE GREAT MAGISTRATE OF ALL

There's nothing that compares to
THE SOVEREIGN GOD on high
to reach up toward
the heavens to
the great high skies
where
THE KING OF KINGS
of Heaven,
Our GREAT LORD
resides.

HE split open both sides,
as HE tended to our cries,
where THE HOLY ONE resides.

HE split open the world
for the sake of HIS creation
from above all sides
for the way to *True Creation*
and took for our transgressions
life's most chosen lessons
and set about HIS holy legislations.
To witness to,
to bear fact, and to solidify the pact.

HE began HIS sessions with
the great high courts
to record and testify
to this LORD GOD on high
that it is true!
HE filled all of what HE has said.
HE fulfilled *The Law*
THE GREAT MAGISTRATE of all.
HE set into motion
with endearing great devotion
as HE set HIS great high motion

Prophetic Utterances

to preserve HIS one true devotion.
HIS *beloved* and HIS *chosen*
HIS church on high
the light is in their eye.
The love of GOD has spoken to
HIS church on high.
Time is nigh.
Look toward the heavens,
you'll see HIS wondrous light
THIS KING of the heavens
THE GREAT WHITE KNIGHT.

The stars all point toward HIM
as they bow in awe before HIM
as they worship and adore HIM.

THE GREAT I AM
THE WONDROUS KING,
THE RULER and MAKER
of everything.

HIS time has come,
since the world began
to show forth HIS splendor
in *The Chosen One*.

THE HOLY ONE OF ISRAEL
would like to announce:

The arrival of HIS SON
THE ONE the world denounced.

As it was written "*In the beginning*"
and written from the start,

HE came to save salvation
with a brand new heart.
HE made the way for this
New Day!!
Because HE chose to obey.

The Cry of His Heart

HE paved the way for this
New Day!!

The highway to Heaven is
about to start for all who have
loved HIM,
the pure in heart.
The Journey has ended.
The Journey to find has arrived
and ended upon,
at last,
This Judgment Day!
Sing *Halleluiah!!!*
The trumpets shall shout.
The sojourning has finished.
We'll sing *Halleluiah* from
start to finish.
The Journey has ended.

Halleluiah!
The road that we traveled
has been traveled all the way.
The things that we forsook
have brought us this way.
As it was said *"In the beginning"*
and we can attest to it
"In the end."

The way that was chosen
was led by
"Our Friend"
The way has been laid
for
This Judgment Day.
THE KEEPER of treasures
since the world began.

THE KING on high
THE KING of the chosen,
THE KING from on high,

Prophetic Utterances

who rules in our heart.
"The reason for the season"
resides in the heavens
and rests in our hearts
and finds joy in the skies.

THE MAKER of all
THE CREATOR on high
HE chose to transform
and thus offered to die.
So we could take love in our hearts
and partake of
HIS GLORY of glories
in HIMSELF.

Psalms 89:18, 2 Peter 1:17

The Cry of His Heart

THE DESIGNER FROM ON HIGH

Took the shape of a man
and allowed HIM to die
and patiently waited for
This New Day!
To be born
to deliver.

THE DELIVERER free from
the scorn,
no longer *mocked.*
No *disgrace* to HIS face
because HE had favor on the
whole human race.

Love is the reason
HE chose to die
and love is the reason
HE reigns from on high.
HIS love is everlasting.
HIS joy is complete.
In death did HE rise again
to accomplish this feat.

THE HOST OF HEAVEN
THE GREAT PRINCE OF PEACE
gave the love of HIS SON
so we all could feast.
"The Feast of The Fools" it once
has been said
is no longer foolish
since sin is dead.

THE LIGHT everlasting
at last is here
as THE PRINCE OF PEACE
did, at last, reappear.

Prophetic Utterances

We sing *"Halleluiah"*
the trumpets resound to:

THE GREAT I AM
THE ALPHA and OMEGA
THE AUTHOR and FINISHER
THE FINISHER OF FINISHERS
and THE PUBLISHER OF OUR FAITH
THE ALPHA and THE OMEGA
THE GLORIOUS ONE

Isaiah 9:6, Hebrews 12:2

The Cry of His Heart

THE GOD

THE GOD from on high
THE GOD who understands
THE GOD who has spoken
THE GOD of our dreams
THE GOD of our realities
THE GOD of the majestic
THE GOD of all

THE PRINCE OF PEACE
THE GOD and THE FATHER
THE NOBLE and TRUE ONE
THE GREAT SHEPHERD
THE SHEPHERD from on high
THE EVERLASTING PEACE
THE HONORABLE ONE

THE GREAT I AM
THE GOD of all comfort
HIS EVERLASTING PEACE
THE FORSAKEN ONE
THE RULER and SHAKER of
"The Great High Society"
THE PRINCE OF TIDES

THE EVERLASTING PEACE
THE GOD who sees
THE GOD who believes
THE GOD who receives
THE GOD who pleads
THE GOD who loves
THE EVERLASTING KING

THE GREAT HIGH CALLING
THE GOD OF CONTRASTS
THE HOLY ONE OF ISRAEL
THE GREAT I AM

Prophetic Utterances

THE ALL FORSAKEN ONE
THE LOVER of my soul
THE GREAT I AM
THE BELIEVER of me
chained to a tree
for all to see
The Call.
For the sake of us all
THE LOVER of my soul
THE GREAT I AM

Romans 15:5, Hebrews 13:20

The Cry of His Heart

MY GOD

It's like YOU are making
music with my mind.
My MAKER of the moment
who motioned from on high
the precepts of the sky.
Who for us—
Chose to die.
HE is the center of my eye.

The War wages
all around me,
inside of me
The War wages
for all the world to see
who know me.

I will fight for my freedom
turning to THE PRINCE
who saves me.
The Battle wages around me
my victory has been won
all because of the things
HE has done.

HE *promised* HE would show
HIS *promise* HE does keep,
for THE GREAT HIGH SHEEP
HE gave HIS life for
just one sheep.

THE GREAT HIGH SHEPHERD
to HIS honor, HIS Word
HE *will* keep
though *The Day* is dawning,
as fresh as the morning dew.

Prophetic Utterances

I think on my BELOVED
and long to be near YOU.
YOUR precepts are lovely
and full of grace
all to save this human race.

Thank YOU for YOUR love
so true.
We just come to worship YOU.
The days go by, our longing deepens
for just the sound
to hear the words that YOU
are speaking.
What great love is this?

The beauty of YOUR kiss
on such a day as this.
THE ANOINTED ONE from on high
YOUR beauty we do miss.

Thank YOU for YOUR one true heart
that healed the broken hearted
that sealed up my tattered
and torn heart.

The beauty of YOUR purpose
The renderings to YOUR Call
YOU healed the chafed and broken
who surrendered to YOUR Call.

The love YOU have with YOU
The love YOU have around YOU
is the arsenal needed to free
all those who are bound.
In love, YOU save and recover
no recompensing too great or small.

The love YOU are made of
lives *inside* of me.
YOUR love has set me free.
In love, YOU chose to deliver.

The Cry of His Heart

With YOUR love, YOU leave YOUR mark,
on our heart YOU do impart,
it is the love that scrolls around us.
The hands of *time* enfold us.

When man could only point
out the spot,
YOU *touched* my tarnished heart.

To YOU be all the glory.
THE MASTER of my mind.
YOU move our hearts with
YOUR words
in the most stately fashion,
as YOU weave the grand design
of the page of the day,
in a rather extraordinary fashion.

Perceiving our perceptions
within trepidations of
wonderful orchestrated bits
of YOUR orate.

Oh, GREAT DESIGNER!
How do YOU dine her?
YOUR Bride clothed in stature.
THE GROOMSMEN awaits.

Song of Solomon 2:8-9, 6:3; Isaiah 1:18

Prophetic Utterances

THE DESIGNER OF MAN

Set YOUR love in motion
like the waves upon the ocean
and inside YOUR
heavenly domain YOU
will find me
to get a glimpse of YOUR
heavenly nature.

Commune with me, while
YOUR awesomeness consumes me.
YOU'RE the desire of my heart!
Although, I only know in part.

YOU whisper sweet *"somethings"*
to me
all the day long until the evening
turns to dawn.
YOU wake me in YOUR own special way
with lyrics inside, they do play
resurrecting anytime of the day.
YOU'RE as close as my nose is to my face
yet, closer than any humanly embrace.

YOUR touch goes much deeper
than words can implore.
YOUR vastness knows no boundaries,
nor surrendering to shores.
YOUR oceans have no barriers
and are not enclosed with doors.
Not a man has explored all YOUR
ocean floors.

YOUR ways are much deeper than
anything known to man
for we are a mere vapor
compared to the deep.

The Cry of His Heart

YOUR horizons are endless
YOUR waves are majestic
YOUR truths are timeless.
YOUR complexity is simply great
YOU'RE *a visionary* first-rate!
How could it be that YOU fashioned
the likes of me?

In the beauty of YOUR HOLINESS,
once did I dwell,
then onward to a single cell.
The division was such
it simply did not deduct
nor cause YOUR creativity to run amuck.

YOU fashioned me in the mystery places
in the unseen—far away from the faces.
YOU chose all the variables
as YOU saw fit, positive and negative
did YOU simply knit
as YOU sculpted away at YOUR plan.
YOU inscribed in my features
ascribed to be teachers
the uniqueness of my being.
The imperfections are asymmetrical
created with a plan
designed by THE DESIGNER
THE GREAT CREATOR of me.

The uniqueness YOU display
is there as a guide to show us the way
to become YOUR Bride.
The imperfect is perfect to
THE DESIGNER of
the plan.

To make the person simply
more than a man.
YOU fashioned as
THE DESIGNER OF MAN

Prophetic Utterances

with the greatest of ease
to yield more to the beholder
than just to please.
To fulfill YOUR purpose in ordinary man
YOU go about with the greatest of ease.

Designing with no intention to please.
It is THE DESIGNER'S delight, *so-to-speak,*
to recall HIS human race
once HE has taken to flight.

To not forget
the great plan
of THE ARCHITECT of man.
To create our features
in opposition to other creatures.
To create in our features
with each one unique.

The symmetry seems balanced as such
until you compare its directional forces
which are beyond our control.
The variety creates unity with a
a special touch
with contrasting rhythm done
with HIS special touch.

HE emphasizes with purpose
as HE proportionally plans
the very last detail of this *"man plan"*
as HE composes contrast with rhythm
and contrast with force.
It is beginning to be quite a discourse.
The directional forces come what may
are designed for a reason for this very day.

To give way to
THE DESIGNER of life.
The shadowy areas all seem
to fit as this was HIS Plan

The Cry of His Heart

as HE started to knit.
HE wove in HIS fragrance
from on high
to entice a certain passerby.

The motion commanded
the emotion to zing!
HE was almost complete
bringing the texture to light
in HIS human being!
The form was centrally complete.
The pattern for man
was really quite chic!
His stature erected clear toward the sky
giving perspective to the untrained eye.
THE VISIONARY of visionaries did not
create just to please.

HE sowed in some contrast to bend
the knees.
While the atmospheric forces
tended to squeeze and embrace
this one man representative of
the whole human race.

THE DESIGNER of grace
HE did implore to keep this man humble,
but not on the floor.
What a distinctly unified theme,
this *thing* called *man* really did seem.
Like any good design
can attest. The harmonious whole
did HE invest.

HE emphasized control to the plan
while designing HIS subordinate
This *thing* called *man*.
The harmony sways in a rhythmical way
dancing in unison as HE created away.

Prophetic Utterances

As
THE GREAT DESIGNER of man
did orchestrate,
as THE HEAD DESIGNER did play,
the *melody of man* took shape.
With the stroke of HIS HAND
HE DID create given with the abilities
to procreate.
HE fashioned HIS likeness
into one man.

Genesis 1:26-27, Ecclesiastes 11:5

The Cry of His Heart

THE GOD OF ALL MIGHT

HE heads the human race
with the touch
of HIS grace.
A wave of HIS hand
HE commands
this *final stand!*

As it was said *"In the beginning,"*
to save THE SON OF MAN.
The Plan is quite grand
it has all been planned.

GOD, come retrieve
YOUR stale and parched land
beckon it back!

The desert and the dry land
declare:

*The earth, the land belong to
the I AM*
THE MAKER of the day
who fashioned out of clay
vessels to HIS Day.

THE POTTER has come!
Let's have some fun and rejoice
with THE KING on bended knee
and the bowing tree,
the blade of grass
for all the world to see.

HE *died* and *rose again* for
the likes of you and me.
THE GOD of the light

Prophetic Utterances

THE GOD of all might
THE RULER of the seas.

Who sought to seek HIS own
brought them to the throne
brought them on their knees,
not ignoring their needs
THE GOD of our peace.

Romans 9:18-26, 1 Peter 5:10-11

The Cry of His Heart

YOU ARE MY DESIRE

Refined by the refiners fire.
Embrace *The Holy Choir*
as we dance
HIS songs of romance.

We'll dance until dawn
all the day long
to the love that was
paid and bought with
the blood of THE LAMB.

*"Save this last lamb for me.
Save this last
dance for ME"*, He said.
*"Save the last dance for my lover
and ME."*

HE said, *"We could enter for free!
Let us swirl among the mountain tops
and imagine we're at all the tree tops"*

We'll be flying so high my KING and I.
HIS desire will be announced
from the chimney tops.
We move with such grandeur
as we sail on our love
to the highest, high places
in love like a dove.
In glory and gentleness
we'll quietly sway,
as we go further and further into
a *New Day*
from glory to glory.

Prophetic Utterances

THE GROOMSMEN has come
for HIS Bride.
HE has guaranteed it'll be quite a time!
To glory we'll go about the land
with THE ONE who loves me
embracing my hand.
HE took me to places so deep
I do not know
and fashioned a new heart of clay.
THE POTTER had HIS way with me
and now I am set free
to be all HE created in me.

HE gave me a gift, so precious and true
HE said, *"I have chosen you,*
you'll be the vessel which carries MY voice.
You are the one
MY one true choice.
We'll go on engagements together
you see, for I desire to be with thee.
So, say what I tell you to say
to them all.
We cannot afford to stall
'The Time' will not tarry!
Very soon we'll be married!"

Oh, what a wondrous awesome day!
GOD has really got a lot to say.
HE is speaking so fast and
poignant to me
desiring to set all HIS people free.
Once they are free,
they will be free indeed.
There will be no need of chatter
because the KING OF HIGH MATTER
came and did take
HIS wife for HIS sake.

Song of Solomon 6:3, Psalms 60:5

THE DAY OF DOUBLE PORTION

For the whole world to see
watch what HE will be doing
for you and me.

The Day is drawing from ME
to fill MY longing of MY children
to THE GREAT HOW ART.

HE is THE RULER and THE MAKER
THE GOD who sees
HE is THE MAKER of the crafter.

Who uses alabaster
to inscribe in their hearts
THE MASTER of *The Call*.

The Game is about to start
get yourself ready.
THE SPEAKER is about to start.

Just wait to see
what I will impart.
It will blow the world apart.

I AM preparing HIS very heart,
for HIS Show is about to start.
The incubation period
is complete.

Psalms 149:2, Revelation 1:1:3

Prophetic Utterances

THE CHURCH IS UNDER ATTACK

I'M calling for "Pastor Jack"
we're in a "State of Emergency"
the whole world is about to see.
We have to take our place.

To protect the human race
the enemy has come
for *The Bride*.
We must rise up and cover her!

Although, this will create a stir
everybody must take their place
to save GOD'S chosen ones
the human race.

The human race is on.
We must stay on the road.
Get in line to pursue to see
HIS glory shine
and witness HIS grand design.

In order to win,
we must step in
and take our stand
every woman and every man.
We're seeking to take the cup.
The relay has begun.

The race is on!
Are HIS people in their place
to reach and grab the baton?
The slightest waver could cost us
the race!

We need the chosen runners
who will fall in line

The Cry of His Heart

to help win the divine.
We must pursue the race to
look up to HIS face.
Spread MY gospel of *LOVE*
sent from above,
which has descended like a dove.

It's the essence of
the beauty of
THE DEITY
for the whole world to see.

Psalms 19:5, Hebrews 12:1

Prophetic Utterances

THE SECRETS OF THE BOOK

The mysteries of the three's
HE'S about to disclose
"The Mystery of the Three"
we have tried to see
just why is there deity.

The world is connected by three
the form is the same,
but not the cover of the look.
What's written in everybody's
spirit is a unified design.

The chapters change,
but the design is MINE.
These are MY people
These people are MINE!
Come look upon MY grand design.

It's time for an authentic look
THE AUTHOR and PUBLISHER is speaking.
Please! Come meet HIM.
HE wants HIS people to enter in
to see what HE is about to announce.

HIS endeavor
"The Secrets of The Book"
It is the best ever!
It's HIS unified design
It's the best of the shows.

THE DESIGNER is about to disclose
"The Secrets of The Book"
so we may get a look
at the life within the line.

The Cry of His Heart

THE CREATOR of the binding,
the covers all are unique.

We're about to hear
from THE AUTHOR.
We have to be there to hear
what HE will share.
"It will cost you something to dine!
But I need
the setters of the show
to do their work below."

To prepare for
THE GREAT AUTHOR of all time
THE CREATOR of all divine.
"The Mystery of Design"
We need variety to entice the world
to see.

Hebrews 12:2, 1 John 5:7-8

Prophetic Utterances

I AM THE AUTHOR

I AM is coming to sign HIS book.
Will you come meet HIM?
I AM the glue that fashioned you.
I AM the glue
which strengthened you.

I AM the glue that purposed you.
I AM the glue who moved you.
I have stuck like glue
pursuing you.

I AM THE KEEPER of the vine.
I AM the life giving force
THE ONE you can't divorce.
MY ink well will never run dry
MY ink never runs out.

I AM the glue who stuck to you
I AM THE ONE who drew you
I AM THE ONE
I AM the keeper of the book
I AM THE GREAT I AM.

I AM the essence of the book
THE WORD is ME
THE WORD is THEE
I AM THAT I AM.

No matter how you spell it
I AM THE AUTHOR and FINISHER
of your faith.
I AM the sea that rages
around you.
I AM the one about
to change you.

The Cry of His Heart

THE KEEPER OF THE VINE
is at the starting line.
The Race is about
to start.

To seek the pure in heart
followed by
The Horse and *The Cart*.
The Horse and *The Rider*
are on their way
down here.

Exodus 3:13-15, Hebrews 12:2

Prophetic Utterances

THE GREAT HIGH GOD

Is redesigning HIS ark
in the dark,
for the sake of the world throughout.

THE MASTER of design
is manifesting *The Divine*
from right under our noses.
The plans for *the ark* are in our hearts
where moth or rust, nor thief can steal.
The plan of THE GLORIOUS ONE.
THE GREATEST DESIGNER
since the world began.
The plans are being drawn as we respond
to HIS VOICE
THE HOLY ONE OF ISRAEL.

THE MASTER ORCHESTRATOR from above
has wooed us with HIS LOVE
sent from up above.
To show all the world what
HE'S made up of,
of all the things Eternal.
Nothing about HIM will spare
because HE'S THE KING OF THE AIR.
HIS Eternal Treasures are rare
kept safe from the salty air.

HIS RUBIES are divine
HIS DIAMONDS turn to wine
HIS EMERALDS all enthrone us
HIS JADE is found within us.
HIS ALABASTER BOX is anointed
and completely appointed
to hold all the treasures that are true
for every woman and man, every girl and boy.

The Cry of His Heart

HE'LL POUR out HIS TREASURES unlimited
regardless of the size of the vessel.
HE'S THE GOD of the impossible
HE'LL do what HE pleases,
despite the appearance, of who we are—
limited by sight.
But they will see HIS gifts eternal
flowing out from me and all HIS people throughout,
from as far as the east is from the west.
HE'LL pour HIS SPIRIT out from the north
and the south.

HIS love will be poured out
like an unending spout.
We'll hardly be able to contain it
for THE SPIRIT is having her way
because it's her day
to pour out from the mouth of it.
Her treasures untold and the wealth of it
to embark on Her royal ship.
To expose Her love to everyone on all sides
and to extol for the whole world to see.

To embrace Her worth.
Set before the earth
and to welcome the upcoming bride.
To see "THE GREAT WEDDING DAY"
set forth from above
in the shape of love.

As HE embraces HIS Bride
from far and wide.
With the most amazing holy stride
from far and wide.
THE KING OF ALL KINGS
will arrive in a holy vessel and chariot.
The Horse and *The Rider* are one.

Prophetic Utterances

The message has been delivered.
I'M coming for
the festival on high
"The Festival for MY Brides."
They are chosen from
far and wide.
They are the delight of delights
to HIS eyes.
THE KEEPER
THE SOJOURNER
of bliss.

It's surely a gala you can't miss
that's sealed with a holy kiss!
Sent from above in the shape of love
from THE FATHER of The Bride.
She is HIS one delight.
For her, HE began HIS flight
to end her final plight.
For her, HE risked it all.

HE allowed all man
to fall—for the sake of us all
who heard *The Call*
and responded to save us all from
the creature who is the
grim reaper of all.

Now, HIS love is safe
enthroned and embraced.
She's on high HIS holy one.

THE FATHER
THE KEEPER OF THE SON
who is THE GREAT I AM.
Who died and rose again
for all the sons of men.

Swing open the gate!
The parade is about to start.

The Cry of His Heart

We'll hear the drum roll
as HE sets out to extol
the beauty of HIS GRACE
and HIS RIGHTEOUSNESS.

The elegance of HIS touch.
HE is in the upper room
far beyond the Moon.
Clear into the universe
so vast we cannot grasp.

The beauty of HIS ELOQUENCE
THE GREAT HIGH MASTER has come
and spared not HIS ONLY SON
for the sake of all mankind.
HE took us for HIS Bride
so we can walk in stride
chosen from far and wide.
HE passed *The Great Divide*
and takes us to
The Great Beyond
HIS love is all around us,
in us and is us.

We are fashioned in HIS love
sent down from above
from *The Sea of Love*
in the shape of I AM.

THE WONDER of the world
THE KING OF THE UNIVERSE
HE'S about to take lead
as we hear HIS voice and follow.
HE'LL take us by the hand
as HE issues
HIS one last command:

*"Lay down all your treasure for MINE
and drink of the holy vine.
Your TREASURE is ready,*

Prophetic Utterances

your VINE has come.
Put down your earthly vessels
you are done!"

It's time to gather and come.
All the ancestors
who went before you,
they really want to meet you
and say, *"Chosen one, we've yearned*
for you and blessed every thought above you."
From THE MAKER of the man
HE pours out HIS love from on high.

Look to the sky!
We're going to *The Great Beyond.*
We'll feast together and dine
and bring forth a new wine.
THE BEAUTY OF HOLINESS dines
with the keeper of the housemate.
Who is royal and benevolent and
shines far and wide.

The beauty of HIS Bride,
whom HE crossed *The Great Divide* for,
sent HIS ONLY SON to die for.
To think it is finally done,
HIS joy at last!
The marriage to the bride
who crossed *The Great Divide.*

Matthew 24:3, 1 Peter 3:20-22

The Cry of His Heart

YOU'VE BEEN COMMISSIONED

For MY glory
to go out and preach MY Story.
Poured out, with love
to your cherished love.

HE is THE GREAT I AM
for all the world to see.
Sing of *alabaster*
the stone of MY choice.
We all should rejoice
from the lay people
to the royal.

I will pour out MY glory
on MY sons and daughters
on this *New Day.*

HE'S about to pour out HIS glory
on HIS sons of glory
so they can
tell their story
sent from above
in the shape of a dove.
So all the people
will gloryat how GOD
poured HIS glory when
they hear what the chosen will say
at the church on the way
The Church of Love
sent from above.

We need to *"vest up"* with HIS armor
to reveal HIS power
that HE will shine
from above

Prophetic Utterances

for the whole world to
marvel and see.

Isaiah 61:1, Colossians 1:28

The Cry of His Heart

THE PRINCE OF THE HIGHWAY

Of The Prophets spoken
HE'S going to impart
so *The Show*
will start in every heart.

THE SPEAKER of *The Show*
is about to go
and make a way for
The Judgment Day.
It could be today.

Call Jack of the hay
and say,
"It could be today!
Prepare the church on the way."

The Race is now starting.
The glory's departing
and is now imparting
in every heart in the
church throughout.
See what HIS majesty
and splendor will look like.

HE is THE GREAT I AM
risen from the grave and
The Great Beyond.
Let's start off this *New Day*.
The Race is underway.

Rejoice at this *New Day*
all MY people of *The Way.*
THE KING of glories
has spoken today.
HE has a lot to say
to the church on HIS way.

Prophetic Utterances

HE is coming today
to visit Jack on the way.
To pour out HIS glory and
reveal HIS story.

Because *The Day of Dread*
is looming overhead.
The Storm is about to start
in the world throughout.

THE PRINCE of The Highway
is the byway to get to
the oceans of love
sent from above
to HIS church with love.

Don't be late!
It's really the date
since the world HE did create.
HE'LL make HIS debut on the chosen
select few.

Daniel 9:26, Matthew 11:21-24

The Cry of His Heart

THE GODFATHER CLOCK

It's the tick tock
that keeps nagging you.
The ringing, pulling in your ear.
It's the *"I'd love to hear your
story ma'am, but
I have somewhere to be,
something important to do.*

*I'd really love to sit and listen
to you state your case,
but there's something calling me
I have to attend to."*

THE ETERNAL MASTER OF TIME
is THE GREAT I AM
HE has requested our service
which will cost us.
We'll have to put our cares
aside regardless of their
importance to us.

They'll have to go behind us,
if HE is to go before us.
Yes, I know your boss just died,
and now you're unemployed.
I know your money is gone and they're
about to turn your electricity off.

Yes, I know your kids are sick
and you need to get them
cough syrup
yes, I know
but, no you don't!

It's getting very late
The Harvest is about to take shape.

Prophetic Utterances

The needs are great
MY sheep won't wait!
They are hungry and starved
will you give them your life?
For MINE?

Will you place your love
of others in the back seat for ME?
Will you risk being late for your
deadline or appointments,
so you can make *the divine* one
at hand?
Will you risk your
image of perfection
even among all
the chosen few who are
called among you?

Will you *please* ME at
the head of the church
and *not* the church ahead of ME?
Will you look for ME?
THE GOD of *The Second Hand*.

Matthew 18:11-14, John 15:13

The Cry of His Heart

THE SELF-MADE MAN

We're really about to awake
there are a lot of lives at stake.
I AM THE GOD who inconveniences
the need won't wait.

The Wedding date has been set.
MY Bride won't wait! Will yours?
THE BRIDEGROOM has a date
The Wedding won't wait.
Will you risk it all
for the sake of MY Call?

"My Time is at hand, I've got to save
my shrine
my image of perfection
and risk being
late for my appointments.
I won't risk looking less than great.
I've got my own schedule.
I can't be flexible."

The first heap is already started,
the flag has been waned.
The Show's begun and
the people are starting to run
for the gold.

They're poor, hungry and fatherless
they're starving, you see.
The need is desperation
they're heading
to cross the finish line
to meet their CREATOR.
The Star of *The Show*
THE HOST OF HOSTS
will issue a toast.

Prophetic Utterances

To all those who laid down their time,
to help bring forth new wine
to meet the need in this
dry dead land.
The Great Time Clock is about to stop.
Will you give ME your time
so you can have MINE?
Will you risk your reputation?
To travel with deprivation, with the outcast,
the shaken, the ones you
wouldn't be caught dead with,
the ones that challenge your reputation
the starving, beat up sheep,
whose covering really doesn't look that neat?

Proverbs 6:16-19, Luke 1:51-53

Prophetic Utterances

PART TWO

Writings from 2012-2014

"And now I have told you before it comes, that when it does come to pass, you may believe."
John 14:29

THE GLORY OF GOD

BEHOLD! The glory of GOD
HE'S majestic, wondrous
to be *magnified*
exalted above
the heavens
marveled at
impressed with
yes, HE'S *amazing!*

THE GOD of the morning
the evening and the night
THE ALPHA and OMEGA
ALMIGHTY GOD
OUR CREATOR
REDEEMER
EVERLASTING FRIEND
OUR GUIDE
OUR DEFENDER
OUR BRIGHT and MORNING STAR.

To be gazed at
to view HIS wondrous light
HIS breaking dawn
HIS morning dew
HIS stars shine bright
THE ARTIST
shines tonight.
HE'S *spectacular*
without end.
Look into HIS splendorous light
as HE
guides you through
this life.
You are never
out of HIS sight.

Prophetic Utterances

HE is your constant companion
day and night.
THE REDEEMER of your
soul has set a lofty goal.
Watch how your life unfolds
as your story is told
to the masses
young and old.

HE has redeemed you with
an outstretched arm
and everlasting grace
to wipe shame off your face
and put love in its place.

THE AUTHOR and
THE FINISHER
of you.
MY precious jewel
who is no fool
but is being used as a tool
in this spiritual school.

We need HIS grace
to help us with *The Race*
without disgrace
to save the human race.

It began with a chase
sometimes HE had
to help us
finish our call
and win the race.
HE slows us down
HE speeds us up
HE causes us to slumber.

To the very end
HE will defend the
helpless little mother.

The Cry of His Heart

HE hears her cries
even her sighs.
HE takes delight in her
the apple of HIS eyes.
It is no surprise
HE chose her
baptized her as the
emblem of HIS love.

HIS endless mercy
lies upon her
for now and for all
eternity
to show her bliss,
the radiance above
in the heavens beneath
HIS majestic and glorious throne
The One
HE rules
all day and all night.

It is HIS delight
to take away all
fright with
HIS mighty might.
THE HEALER,
REDEEMER rules
the heavens
and the earth beneath
HIS wondrous light.

It is HIS delight
to keep the heavens
in HIS sight
all day and all night.
THE ARTIST shines
tonight
to every man, woman
and the Jew
to name a few.

Prophetic Utterances

HE designs the world
for every girl and boy
to usher in HIS glory
as HE finishes off
HIS Story
from glory to glory.

HE'S about to take flight
from the heavens
upright
to set the stage for
HIS wondrous glory.
It is HIS Story
to mankind.
THE AUTHOR and FINISHER
of the people beneath
and beyond
as THIS ONE RENOWNED
puts the gavel down
for the final time.
There will be no crime
no murder and such.
HE'S up to stuff at
record speed
to meet every need
for HIS Church below.

They really are a mess
but HE'S about
to bless,
set free everyone
who is in bondage
and deliver them
and the trouble they
are in so they can win
and enter into
THE LORD OF HOSTS
THE KING OF GLORY
HE who authorized

The Cry of His Heart

The Story of This Creation
of MINE.

It is about time!
HE'LL stop on a dime
to devour the sublime
the shapeless spine
and usher in a blow
and off HE'LL go
and continue HIS *show*.
So all will know
THIS KING OF GLORY
to know HIS message,
HIS Story from
glory to glory.

Get ready, sit still
it's going to be
a thrill, a shrill
to say the least as
HE plunders
HIS enemies at
HIS feet.

They better get ready
to meet their feat as
HE plunders them
under HIS feet.
No one can compete with
THE GREAT HIGH PRIEST
THE ALMIGHTY GOD
THE HEBREW GOD
who isn't at all odd.
HE will shod
HIS enemies with one
single swipe
on HIS chosen night
with HIS splendor
above in the shape
of love.

Prophetic Utterances

HE'LL give a mighty shove
HE'LL come like a dove
from the heavens above
all for HIS *Beloved*,
HIS Church below
to bring them
high up in the sky
before they die.
HE'LL save them forever.
It is HIS endeavor
to redeem HIS own
and bring them home
to the place of glory.
It is HIS Story from
glory to glory
HIS Church on high
HE'LL lift them up in
the sky and draw them
nigh.

You ask why?
To show off
HIS heavenly hosts
and usher in a toast
to the believing few
from every man
woman and Jew
to name a few.

It is HIS delight
to show off HIS site
THIS REDEEMER is all right
HE is a gas
at this great task to save
HIS staff and chosen few
especially the Jew
HIS chosen crew
the apple of HIS eye
they shall have no

The Cry of His Heart

more sigh
as they witness
and glorify HIS Church
on high.

It is why HE brought
them here
because they are
very dear, beloved
adored, revered to
Their MAKER from above.
HE saved them with
HIS endearing love
in the heavens above.
It is what they are made of
a product of HIS love
sent from above
to show off HIS love for
HIS chosen and adored
precious people of THE LORD.

They must know
they are adored by
their MIGHTY LORD
THE MAKER OF HEAVEN
and EARTH.
The Vessels of HIS love
right here on the earth.

HE whistles in HIS love
from up above
in the shape of a dove
from glory to glory.

It is HIS Story
HE'S about to share with
HIS chosen few and
every Jew
to whistle in HIS glory
and tidy up HIS Plan

Prophetic Utterances

The One HE began
The One HE will end
when the time is right.

It will be HIS delight
HE has it in sight.
It will be no fright
but HIS sheer delight
to usher in a *New Day*
it isn't far away.

Hang on! Hold on!
Don't let go!
HE'LL show up for
HIS final cause.
It was finished
at the cross
it's no coin toss.
HE came to save the lost
at all cost.

HE redeemed them at
the cross
so no one would be
lost, left out.
It is HIS glorious delight
to bring HIS Bride
by HIS side
from far and wide.
There'll be no
division from tribe
to tribe.
They will cross *The Great Divide*
and finally be
on HIS side.

HIS beloved and HIS chosen
people on the earth
who found their worth
at *The Message of*

The Cry of His Heart

The Cross
where there is no dross.

It came to life on that day
HE paved the way for salvation,
Eternal glory
That is HIS Story
to show forth HIS glory.
It's fate! It's freedom!
From glory to glory
end of story.

Psalms 29, Revelation 22:16

Prophetic Utterances

THE MESSAGE OF THE CROSS

To save that which is lost
it is no coin toss
it's relevant and real
the biggest of *'big deals'*.

To bring JESUS to the Jews
it is the good news
for all HIS Chosen
Jews.

To bring JESUS to the Jews
it is very good news!
Blessed and purified
no longer paying dues
to the temple of the land.
It was met by HIS hand
pierced for our transgressions
and redeemed by HIS love.

It is the message from THE MAKER.
HE took her out to date her.
The message is from YOUR MAKER.

HE dressed me up and took me
out and shared HIS presence
with me.
HE took me out to write
HIS speech of the night.
It was HIS delight to show
HIS presence on this wondrous
night to HIS chosen and few
every man, woman and Jew
just to name a few.

HIS delight is HIS children
THIS FATHER in Heaven

The Cry of His Heart

is without leaven
purified and glorified and ready
for use.
It is no excuse, nor exaggeration
based on inflation.
No highs and lows
only steady and slow.
It is the way HE goes
through the universe.
There is no curse or curses
anymore
cleaned and purified from
far and wide.
HIS Bride and Chosen One
so they could be by HIS side
from far and wide,
as HE took them in stride
and very wide eyed
to show off HIS Bride
from side to side
far and wide
for glory
for fashion
no rationing in store
it's the economics of heaven.

Psalms 95:6, Isaiah 25:9

Prophetic Utterances

THE WALLS OF INJUSTICE

Take prisoners of war.
They rage against you and vehemently oppose you.
But GOD, THE COMMANDER IN CHIEF
of all heavenly forces is on your side.

HE is coming for HIS Bride from far and wide.
HE wars with you from *The Great Divide*.
HE'S coming for HIS Bride from every side.

The walls of injustice are in pursuit of you.
But *the walls of injustice* are split in two
making a way of escape for you.

You are a chosen vessel, a royal priesthood.
I'VE broken down the wall placed in front of you
they are split in two right before you.

The walls of injustice are split through.
Go ahead and step through the rubble and the ruin
for something is brewing right in front of you.

Something is brewing inside of you.
A new day and a new way
further north is ahead of you.

Psalms 103:6, Proverbs 2:8-9

The Cry of His Heart

A BRAND NEW DAY

A brand new way.
Behold, your KING!
THE KING OF GLORY
continues your story
to show forth HIS glory.

The adventure continues
The Journey resumes.
HE'LL tell you which way to choose,
when *The Journey* is long for some
short for others.

HE orchestrates life like no other.
HE'S THE ALPHA and OMEGA of TIME
HIS stratosphere is very near to you
outside your ear and upon your life.
HE loves you like you are his wife.

HE leads, HE guides, HE also resides
in your heart and in
the heaven's does HE abide.
HE is always by your side.
Walking through the mysteries of life
with you from the far and wide.

HE *can't* be outnumbered.
HE *can't* be outdone.
HE is THE HOST OF HEAVEN
from where all life has begun.
Like the rising sun to the setting moon
HIS ways are majestic even at noon.

HE is THE GOD OF CREATION
THE ROYAL GROOM
allowing life and also doom.
THIS HEAVENLY GLORY

Prophetic Utterances

who goes from story to story
writing and recording
every step of our journey.

HE plans, HE orchestrates
your every move, your very style
to your simplistic groove.
HE'S on the move to keep
you in HIS groove.
HE uses fast and slow rhythms
of style while all the
while HE is defeating denial.

HE loves beyond measure
HIS mercy never ends
HE'S THE GREAT GLORIOUS GOD
forever till the end.
HE is your FATHER who
loves you dearly
for better or worse.

It's quite a discourse
measure for measure
HE plans your way.
HE prepares your day
in an extraordinary way
shading it with love
and laughter, beauty and grace.

HE glides about with
majestic grace and amazing
style all the while
perfecting HIS child
from mile to mile
in your journey of life.

HE perfects your way
and improves your style,
which sometimes
takes a while.

The Cry of His Heart

To improve your style
and eliminate your denial
to lead you to truth in
HIS BELOVED CHILD.

Who is OUR KING from
glory to glory
to tidy up your story
to show forth HIS glory
revealed in you.
HE believes in you
even when you have
doubt.
Doing this in the world
throughout.

Give HIM your hand
Give HIM your heart
Give HIM your confidence
Give HIM your doubt
Give HIM yourself in
the world throughout.

HE'LL lead you and
guide you every
step of the way
through highways
and byways
and crossroads and such.
Through valleys and streams
in visions and dreams and
through mysterious detours.

HE is THE KING OF WONDER
there is no other.
And up steep dark
trails through *The Valley of
Uncertainty*
and mountainous terrain.
While preparing you for battle

Prophetic Utterances

until HIS glorious reign
THE MAJESTIC GOD
THE AWESOME WONDER
of which there is
no other!

Isaiah 33:21-22, Revelation 22:12-17

The Cry of His Heart

HE IS GOD

HE owes no one
an explanation of
HIS doings.

All HE says is,
"Trust ME"
and have faith in ME
I AM THE DRIVER
you are the passenger.

I AM THE PILOT
you are the co-pilot.
We are in this
journey and adventure
together.

Trust ME always
I AM for you,
not against you.
I will deliver you from
trouble.

I will set your feet
on a straight path,
always guiding
and reassuring you
all along the way."

Proverbs 3:5-6, Isaiah 41:9-10

Prophetic Utterances

THE GREAT GARDENER

People sometimes think
they know all the fruit in your life,
like really?
Judge them by their fruit they say!!
But have you ever looked
at a fruit tree and seen
all the fruit at one time?
Impossible!!

For some fruit is hidden
behind other fruit and
some fruit is way underneath,
or way up high
not visible to the naked eye.
Do they know the fruit
saved from only partial decay?

But GOD who sees from every angle
sees all the fruit, the good, the bad
and the not so lovely.
He sees the bruises
from whence they fell
and knows the difference
between bruised fruit
and bad fruit.

HE picks and prunes
as only
"THE GREAT GARDENER"
can and preserves as much
as HE can.
He cuts the fruit open
when necessary,
and cutting to the core
to get a birds eye view.
HE prunes HIS trees

The Cry of His Heart

when the time is right
with divine
precision and skill.
HE knows HIS fruit trees
and HE knows every piece of fruit
and HE alone can
distinguish with taste
HIS fruit
in and out of season!
That's why
HE is THE JUDGE of
the fruit of our lives.

Genesis 1:11-13, Matthew 3:8

Prophetic Utterances

THE ENEMIES OF GOD

They thought they were invincible,
smarter than the best,
truly hidden in their deeds.
But GOD has been watching their
every move and will come
at HIS appointed time,
when they least expect it
and eradicate them from
their hiding places.

With HIS lethal overpowering
Spirit driving them out of their
hiding places,
while they are running and scurrying
about.
Thinking they are getting
away,
only to come to their
final end,
as they are overcome
by a power greater than.
themselves.

This is how it will be
in *The Last Days*
for all the enemies of GOD.
As they are running
in fear and trembling,
thinking they are getting away,
suddenly, death overshadows them,
as they pile upon one another
laying in heaps upon the land.

No longer able to deceive
or hide their abuse of limited power,
in their offices of authority.

The Cry of His Heart

They have succumbed to a power greater
than themselves.
They have met their MAKER
who has all authority,
all power over all principalities.

THE GOD
OF THE ARMIES
OF HEAVEN and EARTH
HE alone outnumbers the rulers
of darkness and perpetrators of shame.
HE will expose them in the open places,
above ground for all to see
their acts of iniquity on humanity,
their injustice, disgust, their former lusts
and acts of betrayal.

"VENGEANCE IS MINE," Says,
THE LORD,
"I WILL REPAY!"

YOU make all things right in
the end.
How we eagerly await,
THE KING OF JUSTICE
to make all the crooked things
straight.
This is nothing to placate.
It is HIS royal date with
the king of darkness to
set him straight at *Hell's Gate*.
It is his fate, and it will not be late.

Deuteronomy 32:35, Psalms 7:11, 68:21

Prophetic Utterances

THE END DRAWS NEAR

The end draws near
like the rising sun to the setting
moon which disappear.

The end draws near
like the drops of rain on
the terrain.

The end draws near
like the setting sun to show forth
HIS glory from which the
the world has begun.

The end draws near
like every tear brought on
by fear.

The End is near.
Whom shall I fear?
But, GOD ALMIGHTY
THE MAKER OF THE UNIVERSE
who is about to make
HIS final discourse.

Whom shall I fear?
But, THE ALPHA and OMEGA
THE BEGINNING and THE END.

Whom shall I fear?
But, GOD ALMIGHTY and
THE ONE whose blood
was shed.

Whom shall I fear?
But, HIS righteous spear
thrown about
the atmosphere.

The Cry of His Heart

Whom shall I fear?
But, GOD alone.

The end draws near
like the fading sky
underneath the watch
of a waiting eye.

The end draws near
why?
It's about THE ONE
whose blood was shed.
HE leads the host of heaven
and it's their blood HE'S about
to shed.

The End Times are here.
Draw near while you
still can.
HE died for every woman
and every man.

HE is THE GREAT I AM
whose sovereign plan
is targeting HIS *Divine Plan.*

HE'S in search of
every man.
It is HIS *Divine Will
and Plan*
to save the lost
before they die.

Before HE rides from
the heavens
throughout the sky.
HE'S in search of
the apple of HIS eye,
you and I.

Prophetic Utterances

HE is Our PRIZE!
Our SAVIOR and REDEEMER
who died for you and I.
You are the desire of HIS heart
from the world throughout.
HE seeks HIS Bride
from every side
to bring them home
straight to HIS Throne.
You are
the apple of HIS eye.
The very reason
HE *chose* to die
was to save you and I,
before we shall die.

So, look up to Heaven
HE'LL come with *a shout*
everyone will hear it,
in the world throughout.

There will be *no doubt*
NO lingering of thought
NO wavering question
NO lingering question,
in the world throughout.

HE is THE HOST OF HEAVEN
who is about to leaven
all sinful intention
by divine intervention.

To show forth HIS glory
from story to story
to glory to glory.

HE rules from the heavens
and reigns in our hearts.
HE'S about to take HIS stand,

The Cry of His Heart

for every woman and every man,
from where all life began.

HE is THE LAMB
THE LAMB that was slain
who was put to shame
and who was blamed
to be the sorcerer
of man.

HE is about to make
HIS stand in defense
of HIS Name.

There is no shame upon
this once MAN
who shed HIS blood
for every man.

HE is A KING
THE KING from on high
who *chose* to die
for you and I.

It is HIS Story
to show forth HIS glory
from story to story,
in the world throughout.

There is *no doubt.*
There is no shame in
THIS MAN
GOD made
THE SOVEREIGN LAMB,
on which all salvation
was placed and pierced
for our transgressions
to give us a lesson.

Prophetic Utterances

From THIS GREAT TEACHER
on high
who *chose* to die
for the likes of you and me.

However unworthy,
however transgressed,
in HIS Name we are
all so blessed.

To come to HIS Throne
and worship and adore
THIS MAN, GOD
chose to die for the likes
of you and I.

THIS GOD called
Man
THIS MAN called
GOD

You better climb aboard.
The Time is at hand.
HE'LL fly from the heavens
with HIS host of the heavens.

And seek out the lost
and save all
HIS chosen vessels
from every part of the land
with HIS sword
in HIS hand.

HE'LL take HIS stand
on Mount Zion and
HIS chosen land,
as HE redeems HIS
chosen ones and
HIS land.

The Cry of His Heart

For now, and all eternity
HE'LL reign from on high
THIS KING OF GLORY
who *will* finish
HIS Story
for now, and forever
and all eternity reign.

Amen and amen

Proverbs 1:7, Luke 12:4

Prophetic Utterances

THE MAJESTIC WARRIOR

THIS GREAT HIGH GOD
to which every knee will bow
and every head
will nod.

They'll bow before
HIM, worship and
adore HIM.
THE KING OF KINGS
for which salvation brings
you home.

To show you
the glory of HIS Throne.
*So, don't wait
too long!
The Show* is about
to start
in the world throughout.

Jump aboard
while you can.
While there is still
time to save you
and restore you
before *The Day*
comes—
*when destruction
and doom is declared
upon the land and
its inhabitants*
by
THIS WATCHFUL GROOM.

HE will sweep you
out with HIS divine broom

The Cry of His Heart

removing all the
waste and debris
from this land
which is going to
start soon.

Hold On! Hang On!
It's going to be
quite a ride as
HE swings from
the heavens like the
TARZAN OF HEAVEN.
Saving HIS loved ones
from the impending
doom of the land.
The Destruction is at
hand.

Climb aboard before
it's too late!
Take your place
by HIS side
while you still
can.

HE *loves you*
beyond measure.
You're *the reason*
HE died.
Please join HIM
as HE marries
HIS Bride
from far and wide
from every side.
It's a royal date,
a royal time
for THIS KING OF KINGS
who comes with a
royal stride.

Prophetic Utterances

There is none like HIM
nor ever will be,
THIS
MAJESTIC KING OF WONDER
HIS MAJESTY!

Climb aboard, there
is still time.
Come join the party
partake and dine
at HIS royal table
with majestic wine.

You've been invited
to wine and dine.
It's *The Show* of all shows
with wonder galore.

You have no idea
just what is in store
for the ones who
are chosen who show
forth HIS glory
from story to story.

HE'LL reign from
the heavens and rule in
our hearts.
HE'S in search of HIS
loved ones
in the world throughout.

Climb aboard
it's getting late
there's not much time
ahead for this royal
date.

Head for *The Ship*
before it leaves dock.

The Cry of His Heart

The Ark of GOD
is gathering HIS flock.

Climb aboard
before it gets dark.

Climb aboard
before the ship
sets sail,
every man and woman
every boy and girl.

Climb aboard
The Ship is about to set sail.
HE'LL bring you to
freedom,
instead of to jail
and *The Lake of Fire*
of which there is
no end.
Which side will you choose?
The choice is yours
you don't have much
time
choose wisely, MY friend.

I give you life, glory
and beauty without end.
The opposite is true
on the other end.

The choice is yours.
It's in your hands
whichever way
you choose,
you win
or lose.

There is no draw.
It is *The Law of Eternity*
for one and for all.

Prophetic Utterances

I hope to see you
this side of heaven.

The choice is yours,
to see MY FATHER
in Heaven.
HE *knows* who you are
HE *knows* you by name.

This is *not* a game
or a stroke of luck;
it's the tick tock of heaven
the stroke of heaven.
The Ship is about to dock.

I'VE issued MY warning,
I'VE sounded the alarm,
I'M preparing for
battle just as I
have planned.

This is more than
a story or mere
poetry.
It is life and death
being presented to you.

Which way will you
choose?
The choice is up to you.
It's in your hands
now.

There will be no one
to blame.
You have been warned
by
The Heavenly Horn.

Which way will you
choose?

The Cry of His Heart

The choice is yours
to either win or lose.

Choose wisely, MY friend.
We are very near *The End*.
The Show's about to
start in the world
throughout.

Times of uncertainty,
storms galore,
prepare for battle.
We are about to go
to war!

The Time is at hand
The land will be struck.
It will be more than
bad luck!

It will be perilous and
panic filled
quaking with fear and
trembling ahead.

The Day of Doom and Dread
is leering just ahead.

There will be wars
and famines
in the world galore.
It will be difficult
to shop
in your local store.

The War will be
waging.
THE AVENGER will
pour HIS indignation
on man.
Take the escape

Prophetic Utterances

while you still can.

Time is wasting
it's about to run out.
People will be screaming
in the world throughout.

There will be no word
of comfort from Heaven
above, just
fierceness of wrath
poured on those
throughout.

Don't say, *"I have
never been warned,
no one took the time!"*
You have had your
chance,
you have had much
time
to hear *the news*
and make up your
mind.

THE FATHER of all time
is preparing for supper
for those who
will dine.
The dinner bell
has rung.
The ushers and servers
have been called.
The Time is coming
for one and for all.

Which way will
you choose?
Which way will

The Cry of His Heart

you end?
In paths of glory?
Or in fires with
no end?

The choice is yours
in the end.
I hope to see you
when I reign from on high.
"Remember, you're
the apple of MY eye
the love of MY life
for all eternity, without
end."

I love you with a love
from on high.
MY love is unending
MY *wrath* is pending.

Choose life
while you still can.
The choice is at
hand.
Till we meet again,
MY child.

I long for your
love and long for your
hand.
It's time to say goodbye
now.
The Warning has been
issued.
The Warning bell rung
I wait for you earnestly.

It is the cry of MY heart.
I long for you endlessly, MY child.

Prophetic Utterances

To present you to THE FATHER
who reigns from on high
HE's quite THE GOD
who made you and I.

Psalms 9:7-8, Ezekiel 38:18-23

The Cry of His Heart

THE FATHER OF HEAVEN

THE FATHER OF LIGHTS
THE GOD OF THE HEAVENS
in which the world
delights.

HE is majestic beyond
wonder,
beyond knowing
beyond end.
HE is waiting to greet
you
because you are
MY friend.

HIS love knows no
boundary.
HIS love never ends.
HE is THE GOD OF THE UNIVERSE
THE GOD OF NO END.

HE is THE ALPHA and OMEGA
OF TIME without end.
THE GOD of all wonders
THE GOD of all time
THE GREAT GLORIOUS GOD
of all that was and is to come,
from where all life has
begun,
from the foundations of
the Earth to the
Sun.

HE is THE GOD OF GLORY
and glories and glories,
and wonders galore,
of *riches* beyond

Prophetic Utterances

measure and *wealth*
beyond compare.

Of all truth and virtue
and awesome wonders
in store,
of majestic turbulences
of heavenly galore
of shooting stars
and galaxies and
way, way more.

Of awesome wonder
and amazing feats
of victory, and
dominion of every kind.

It's the reason
you've been invited
to dine.
To gaze upon
HIS MAGNIFICENCE
and splendor to breathe
in and savor HIS
majestic flavor.

THIS GOD—
THE
ONLY TRUE GOD
of majestic heights,
delights more than
ever to restore and
recapture,
the love of HIS saints
on this pending date.

For the love of GOD
for the love of all
HE is OUR GOD.

The Cry of His Heart

Our AWESOME WONDER
Our BRIGHT and MORNING
STAR
Our ELUSIVE GOD OF MYSTERY
Our ETERNAL DAD
Our HOLY FATHER
Our HEAVENLY HOST
Our GOD OF THE UNIVERSE
Our GOD OF ALL.

This awesome
KING OF WONDER
is about to start
HIS Show.
HE'S been preparing
for centuries, since
the beginning of time.

THIS ONE MAN BAND
THE ORCHESTRATOR of
Man
has lifted HIS hand.
HIS melody is starting
HIS glory is sung
in the hearts of
HIS humans
HIS melody of love.

HE sings with exuberance
HE sings with HIS style
HE sings with heavenly
hosts for miles and miles.
HE is the melody of man.
HE is the melody of me.
HE is the melody of victory
for every bended knee.

HIS love knows no measure.
HIS truth knows no end.
HE'LL lead us to truth

Prophetic Utterances

by THE ONE we call
our friend.
JESUS, OUR SAVIOR,
HIS BELOVED SON.

THEY are CO-CONSPIRATORS
of *This Journey* we've
been on.

Planned from the beginning,
till the end of time
THE FATHER and SON
have delighted to
dine
with the saints
from all time.
It is THEIR desire
THEIR mysterious course
to end
This Mysterious Discourse.
THEY are hand in
hand shouting "Victory!"
from above
with THEIR HEAVENLY
DOVE.
THEY are all called
"LOVE"

Every one of THE THREE
who have spoken to
our hearts and mind
from above.

So it's time to take
your stand,
every girl and boy
and woman and man.
THE MAJESTIC THREESOME
Is issuing a command:

The Cry of His Heart

"Come one, come all!
It's time to dine
with new wine!"

And muster in and savor
this divinely new
flavor
of heavenly glory,
from THEIR
spicy story
of *Life Ever After
and Mercy Without
End*.

Sent from THE FATHER
and OUR BELOVED
FRIEND
THE GOD OF THE UNIVERSE
with HIS SON by HIS side,
HAS sent an invitation to
HIS Bride from far
and wide.

*"It's time to get on
board.
The Meal is about
to start for those
who have sacrificed
in the world throughout.*

*They have been devout
in their search from
throughout.
It's time to finish
up their story
from glory to glory."*

Prophetic Utterances

The End is at hand
your MAKER now stands!
The Warning has
been issued:
HIS *final command!*

It is *now* finished!
The world will *now*
see
HIS AWESOME WONDER
uniquely displayed in
you and me.

Bless you all, bless you all
in the world throughout.
There's no time for
shame and doubt.

Prepare yourselves for
what is at hand,
sounding the alarm
to the worn and down.
HIS MAJESTY IS COMING!
Get going, start running!
It's not time to placate!
The royal date
has been set.
Get your armor
on
The Battle has begun
The War is at hand
armor yourselves up,
all over the land.

THE COMMANDER IN CHIEF
of all armies has
thrust open all heavenly doors,
of all wars upon wars
and perilous times.

The Cry of His Heart

With trouble
upon trouble of every
kind just ahead.
The War is now starting.
Prepare every man
Prepare all you people
Prepare all you land.

THE WAR of THE AVENGER
will soon be at hand
taking captivity *"captive"*
and cleaning
the space.

Getting the place ready
for a brand new race.
Get ready! Get set!
Get ready!
Go!

There's a *New Day*
dawning on the earth
below.
Get ready for battle
on the earth below!

Joel 2:1-5, James 1:17-18

Prophetic Utterances

FOLLOW HIS LEAD

GOD is definitely
ushering in a New Day
a battle cry
prophetic utterances,
prophetic glories
which await us.

The cry of HIS heart
for HIS children,
an ultimatum of sorts,
of the coming days.

We *must* understand
our authority as believers.
We *must* sound
our own warning
to the church at large.

Now is the time
for preparation for battle.
It's the battle cry of our
COMMANDER IN CHIEF.
The time for preparation
is now!

GOD will lead me
to write about
what HE wants shared,
as it pertains to
HIS Story of salvation
and redemption.

HIS *Love Story* to
the masses.
It will surely surface, as
HE has risen from the grave.

The Cry of His Heart

The stories of death will bring
new life to those living.
It is HIS purpose.
It is HIS Will.

Ephesians 6:10-20, 1 Corinthians 15:12

Prophetic Utterances

HIS ACT OF LOVE TOWARD US

The shedding of HIS own blood
and dying on the cross
was just no ordinary thing
or another ordinary day,
when HE accomplished this
extraordinary feat!

It's not like,
"Oh, I think I'll just be beat up
today, be completely pummeled
by man for no reason,
and then be slowly killed
as they all watch,
as MY blood oozes out
of every crevice and orifice
of MY body.

Ah, no big deal…
Then after I DIE,
MY DADDY, "ABBA"
will resuscitate and
bring ME back to life,
so I can mingle with
the disciples.

And oh, yeah…
that sin for which
I DIED,
That's no big deal!
Sin away…..
Sin, sin, sin, sin, sin again.

What I did was for sport,
don't you know!
Mere entertainment!!"

The Cry of His Heart

How dare we!
Hold HIS LIFE
HIS SACRIFICE for our sin
so lightly,
to esteem it as if
it is our right
to keep on keeping on.
Trampling HIS amazing feat,
HIS accomplishment
under our dirty little feet.

It's like throwing dirt,
mud and spitting
on HIM every time
we go back to our dirty
pigpen lifestyle.
Then we snort our way
back to our church pew
full of dirt and grime,
singing *"Halleluiah!!*
Praise The Lord!!"

We have dirtied HIS offering,
giving HIM our new blemishes
of sin, and covered HIM
in disgrace, dishonor
and reproach.
We have put to shame
this GLORIOUS MAN
OF GOD.

This holy, revered
SON OF GOD
without spot or blemish.
We add insult to injury to
THE SON OF GOD,
THE LAMB WHO WAS SLAIN
and we do the same thing every
time we fall from grace.

Prophetic Utterances

We defile HIM and
HIS HOLY NAME.
We bring reproach
to OUR MAKER
and make a mockery
of HIS laying down
HIS life for us,
as if it were no big deal.

It was a big deal!
It cost HIM—
HIS LIFE!
HIS comfort
of Heaven.
HIS songs of adoration,
praise from HIS angels.
The warmth
and spiritual closeness
to HIS FATHER.

HIS *glory*
for our *shame*
HIS *godliness*
for our *ungodliness*
HIS *honor*
for our *dishonor*
HIS heavenly *embrace*
for our *shame* and *disgrace*.

HIS *life*
for our death
HIS *everything*
for our *"nothingness,
unworthiness,
selfishness, ungodliness
and unrighteousness"*
HE gave HIS all.

The Cry of His Heart

All of HIS *worthiness*
for our *worthlessness*,
and He paid a high ransom
for a poor penniless soul.
Who does this?
Any ordinary man?
No! But
an EXTRAORDINARY GOD!

Who loves without end,
whose mercy
endures forever.
Who, but
THE GOD OF THE UNIVERSE
THE MAKER of all things
OUR HEAVENLY FATHER
who adores us so, so much.

HE was willing
to forego
HIS BELOVED SON
so we could live,
and not die and fry.
HE loved us
and still loves us
everyday.

Every moment on our way
back home to HIM,
where *"Freedom reigns*
in liberty
and justice for all"
who enter in
through that still
small gate,
and seek HIS face.

Who seek to know HIM,
to worship and adore HIM,

Prophetic Utterances

to applaud HIM
and to one day
reside with HIM
all eternity long.

HE wants us to walk beside
HIM, to follow HIS leading
as the *good* and *faithful*
SHEPHERD,
not to trample over HIM
doing it our way,
with our lack of style
and finesse.

HE wants our hearts,
and our minds.
Our love is divine
to HIS heart and soul
and HIS heavenly abode.
HE wants us to seek HIS face
so HE can in turn
see our face
from glory to glory.

It's why HE'S written
HIS Story
to show forth
HIS glory
for now and forevermore.

Come, let us dust off
our feet
and have a walk
worthy of our GOD
and HIS PRECIOUS, PRICELESS
TREASURE, HIS SON
"JESUS THE CHRIST"
THE RISEN KING OF GLORY
who continues
to write *our story*

The Cry of His Heart

until we reign with
HIM in glory!

Luke 22:19-22, Hebrews 10:29-31

Prophetic Utterances

I HAVE ORDAINED YOU

I have ordained you
from before the world began.
Ordaining you to go and preach
the good news
to the poor in heart
and in spirit,
for the reviving of their soul.

It was why you were created,
why you were born.
To go forth from story to story
to show forth MY GLORY,
to the hurt and the wounded,
downtrodden believer
and unbeliever.

To give them hope
and a promise of redemption.
It is MY CAUSE
for which you have been appointed.
To reach broken hearts
and broken lives,
bring healing
to their wounded
and bruised soul.

It's why you were born,
to help the hurting,
to bind up their wounds
and speak life
to their dead parched soul.
To guide them to life eternal,
life everlasting
and life forevermore.

The Cry of His Heart

It is *Your Call*—
Your rite of passage from
The Throne Room of GOD,
to display HIS glory
in your debauched story.
To point them to
THE MAKER of all things,
both in Heaven and Earth
from church to church.
Spreading hope and giving glory
to THE KING of HIS Story
from glory to glory,
renewing and igniting
their light shown from above
from THE HEART OF LOVE
and CONVICTION
from *"Heaven's Kitchen."*

THE GREAT CHEF from on high
has commissioned from
HIS heavenly kitchen
good graces to all,
tasty treats from above,
heart shaped in love,
soups of savory flavor,
and ramen's of love
with extraordinary flavor.

Isaiah 61:1-3, Jeremiah1:5

Prophetic Utterances

HE HAS ISSUED A CHARGE

Get into our places
cause JESUS IS COMING
to take from the world HIS OWN.
HE is going to take us HOME.
It is HIS Plan.
"When will this be fulfilled?"
When HIS divine date
and will collide.
Not for us to decide.

It is *The Mystery of The Ages.*
We must prepare to live
and prepare to die.
For no one knows
when *the angel of death*
will come knocking
at the door of our hearts,
the door of our minds.
When it is our time,
it is our time.
Now, bear in mind,
The Eternal Clock
is ticking every second
of the day, every hour
on our way,
every moment
of the day,
as HE sends us on
our way.

The Highway of Heaven
is ushering a call,
"Come one, come all"
there is no time to stall.
HE died to save us all

The Cry of His Heart

from eternal division,
from a life not worth living
to life eternal
sent by THE GRANDFATHER,
GOD, THE FATHER of all.

Ecclesiastes 3:1-2, Acts 10:42

Prophetic Utterances

HIS PLAN

It is HIS Plan
HIS unique design
HIS heavenly landscape
that is about to take shape.
HE musters, HE plans
HE maneuvers each man,
like a piece on a chessboard
across every land.
It is HIS divine plan
for every person, every man.

To prepare them
for battle across the land.
The Battle is waging
The War has begun as
THE FATHER has spoken
to HIS BELOVED SON.
There will be no more decay
from henceforth and now.
HE'S putting a muzzle on every cow
as HE plunders the earth
and turns around with HIS plow.
The Time is at hand for
everyone now.

HE'S issued HIS royal decree
so we should *drop to our knees*.
THE KING OF THE UNIVERSE
is about to spree.
To spree from the heavens,
to the earth below.
HE really only knows
which way HE will go.
TIME is in HIS hands;
HE holds the earth in HIS heart

The Cry of His Heart

HE loves beyond measure
in the world throughout.
This GOD called MAN
This MAN called GOD
is preparing HIS Show,
for the earth down below.

HE'LL orchestrate from heaven
on the earth below,
telling each one
the way they should go.
HE'LL lead them
and guide them
to their gates and
shoot from HIS shotgun.

The Race is taking place
across the land in every
woman and every man.
HE is THE HUSBAND
in search of HIS Bride
from every corner of Earth
to take them to HIS side.
HE'LL usher a sound
and present a blow,
from this side of Heaven
on the earth below.

It is HIS royal race
written on each face,
on the earth below.
Before we know it,
it'll be time to go
to be with THE FATHER
with THE SON
by HIS side
as THEY stroll through
the heavens
walking hand in hand.

Prophetic Utterances

THEY'LL rule from the heavens
and across the world
down below.
It's going to be amazing!
A never-ending show
A show of exuberance
The Show of all shows
The love of our MAKER
as HE starts to dance.

HE'LL dance in the heavens
and in all our hearts.
HE'LL dance in our hearts
and everywhere.
HE'LL dance before
HIS FATHER
for all the world to see.
HE'LL dance HIS glory dance
for everyone to see.
HE'LL dance and sing
*"Glory, Glory to Our GOD
and Our KING!"*
It's going to be quite
a sight to see.

THEY'LL sing in unison
THEIR song of love,
as THEY reign from
heaven above.
THEIR love is never-ending
THEIR mercy is great
THEY love with eternity
written on THEIR plate.

THE MASTER
has issued a toast
straight from Heaven:

*"There will be no more sorrow
or unleaven from Heaven*

The Cry of His Heart

*THE BREAD OF LIFE,
has spoken from Heaven."*

HE loves beyond measure.
HE'LL even out the score,
as HE knocks on the hearts
of all HE adores.

HE reigns supreme
throughout all the land.
HE died and rose again
for every woman
and every man,
every boy and girl
throughout the world.
HIS love is unending
HIS mercy is great
HIS date is taking shape.
Climb aboard before
it's too late!
HE loves you
beyond measure.

Nahum 1:2-3, John 6:32-40

Prophetic Utterances

THE DEMISE OF SATAN

HE'LL even the score
on your enemy below
who—
you all deplore.

HE'LL put him in his
place for all his race,
and reduce his
poignant smile.
His pride of every color.
His hold on the dollar.
He is really such
a deceiver and quite
the liar.
His deception knows
no end.
His lying never ceases.
He goes about and
does what he pleases,
wreaking havoc below.

He's *the heartbreak of heaven,*
unsavored and unleavened.
Deception is his lifestyle.
Death and dread are his
dance.
He has broken many hearts
I'VE heard it on their
knees.

He's *the heartbreak of heaven
the eternal dross*
from where all killing comes.
He's in search of the lost.
He pays no attention
to MY HOLY CROSS—

The Cry of His Heart

only to his deceptions.
Never, MY REDEMPTION!
It's all counted a loss!

He's *the deceiver of
deceivers*
in the world across.
He blames, he cusses
he always fusses
at you and ME,
while he throws
his punches.
He never asks for
direction or permission
from Heaven.
He goes about destroying
and leveling
all hopes and dreams,
without a care.
He takes no mind to
you all out there.
His mind is bent
on destruction,
on murder and
such.
He's the one
who is the cause
of all "*bad luck.*"
He steals the show
on the earth below,
but only for a short time.

He'll be put in his
place of demise
and waste
for all his tactics
on the world below.
He'll pay the price
in *hellfire* below.

Prophetic Utterances

He'll pay for all time,
for eternity and more.
He'll pay for his
miseries he did impart
his disservice on Mankind
in the earth throughout.
He'll pay for the sicknesses
he did inflict on helpless
men and women without
giving a flip.

He'll pay for deceiving every
man, woman and child
across the world
mile by mile.
He'll pay the price
for breaking your heart,
stealing your hope
leaving you on the
ground trying to cope.
He'll pay the price for
his deceptions below
waging *war* on
MY people on the
world down below.
He'll pay the price
this is for sure!
He'll burn everlasting,
receive chastising
from THE GOD OF THE HEAVENS
THE GOD OF THE EARTH
THE GOD OF THE CHOSEN
who are in heaven above
and in the earth below.
He'll pay for his crimes
against humanity at large.

He'll be issued:
MY WARFARE

The Cry of His Heart

MY ETERNAL CHARGE;
he'll eat fire and brimstone
as his main course meal.
He'll be plundered and
punished for his every
steal.
He stole from MY body,
MY chosen ones below.
He'll pay the penalty
for stealing the show
for waging war
against MY beloveds
on the earth below.

I'VE kept their tears
and their sorrows in
MY hand.
I will Issue MY
command and take
MY STAND!
Saving MY children
from his hand at last!
And punishing
the perpetrator,
while I *shall* laugh!
I'LL have the last
word in *this Story*
of MINE.
I'LL fix his wagon
this is for sure!
He'll no longer be
bragging of his
ills and his curse.
He'll be thrown in
the fire of hell
down below,
while I take MY
Reign
on the earth below.

Prophetic Utterances

He'll be in his place,
while I AM in MINE.

I'LL reign in victory
for all the world to see
and save MY children
from
the enemy of loss!
They'll reign with
ME;
every eye shall
see as WE sing
The Song of Victory
from sea to sea.
*"We'll be so happy,
so happy We'll be
when We're finally
united in harmony."*

So, it's time to get
ready.
It's TIME
to start to prepare
yourselves in the
world throughout.
MY Time is at hand
MY Show's about to
start in MY chosen
pure vessels,
in the world throughout.
Prepare your hearts,
your minds and such.

Romans 16:20, 1 Peter 5:8-9

The Cry of His Heart

MY SECOND COMING

Is approaching nearer
than you think.
Prepare your hearts,
in the world below.
I'LL show you which
way you should go.
I'LL lead you
all the while,
preparing for
MY blow.

The trumpet sound
of Heaven
will announce:

*"The arrival of MY SON
whom the world
denounced."*

HE'LL be
THE KING ETERNAL
forevermore,
ruling in power
and authority galore.
HE'LL reign in majesty
and glory and such.
HE'LL even out the score
for every man, woman
every girl and boy.

It'll be HIS joy
to restore all HIS vessels
to honor and more.
Cleaning off their plate,
of the crumbs of decay.
HE'LL fill them

Prophetic Utterances

with laughter and joy
from above.
It's how HE displays
HIS *Royal Love.*

HIS love is everlasting
HIS mercies never
end.
HE bought us back
To HIM by THE ONE
we call FRIEND
HIS SON of Eternity
and all that is grand.

HE'S THE SOVEREIGN
KING ETERNAL
all across the land.
It is time to take
your place.
It's coming to an end
MY human race.

The starting gates are closing
The stands are emptying.
It's time to get ready
The Story is ending.
A new chapter's
about to arrive in
HIS *"Book of Life
and Eternal Living."*

Written from Heaven
with holy hands.
THE AUTHOR is finishing
The Story of Man
HE'S ushering in a *New Day*
and *New Plan*
for every girl and boy
every woman and
man.

The Cry of His Heart

We'll have life eternal
with joy never-ending.
It is "the happy ending"
In HIS *Book of Life*.
HE loves us all so dearly.
Love each other in
the same.

It's no time to bicker,
judge, or to blame.
Prepare your hearts
every one and all.
THE KING'S about to
enter into this foreign
land.
It's time to stand
as HE makes HIS debut
in the heart of HIS children
to make them anew.
HE'LL fix all their cracks.
They're beaten and
they're bruised.
HE'S ushering in
some really *good news!*

The Time is at hand.
Preparation is now!
It has been ushered
by HIS eternal plow
to make straight what
is crooked.

To turn over the dross,
to dig up new soil
with very little toil,
with the *very* heartbeat
of heaven, every stroke
from OUR MAKER.
It's about to take shape
on this *Royal Cruise Ship*

Prophetic Utterances

that's about to set
sail.

The Battleship is
being dismantled.
The Hardship is coming
to its final land.
The Cruise Ship of Heaven
is docking in our hearts.
The sails are full mast.
It's going to be a blast.
It's TIME—
Get ready!
Before I make MY debut—
Get yourself ready!
Every one of you!

Matthew 24:27-51, 1 Corinthians 15:51-58

The Cry of His Heart

THE DAY OF PREPARATION

It's
THE DAY OF PREPARATION
across the land
for every girl and boy.

It's
THE DAY OF PREPARATION
for every woman and
every man.

It's
THE DAY OF PREPARATION
it's time to take your
stand.

It's
THE DAY OF PREPARATION
before I land.

It's
time to get ready.
Prepare your hearts and
minds before I get
down below.

It's
THE DAY OF PREPARATION
The Time is at hand.
I'M coming for MY Bride
in a royal stride.

It's
THE DAY OF PREPARATION
for you and I.

Prophetic Utterances

I am preparing for battle
to battle for MY Bride.

It's
THE DAY OF PREPARATION
The Day is at hand.

Joel 3:9, 2 Timothy 2:19-26

The Cry of His Heart

THE DAY OF THE LORD

That has been spoken of,
by MY chosen
land.
Its inhabitants are MINE
I'M coming for them
all.

The Day is at hand for
one and for all
I'LL reign KING ETERNAL
in every heart of every
man.

"I'm coming at Last!"
To take MY official stand.
The Day is at hand
get ready or *not!*

It is OUR *Royal Plot*
being fulfilled in
OUR time since before
the world has begun.

WE are coming for
OUR chosen ones
from across the land.

The Day is at hand.
Get ready, man!
I'M coming for
MY chosen ones
across the land
Get ready!

I'M issuing a command
all across the

Prophetic Utterances

land.
Time is a wasting
The Time is at hand,
to prepare your
hearts and minds.
It's MY Final Command:
PREPARE!
The Battle is at hand!

Zephaniah 1:2-1; 2:1-3, Zechariah 8:3

The Cry of His Heart

IT'S TIME FOR YOU

O LORD, to reappear—
It's got to be breaking YOUR heart
all the cries of YOUR people,
in the world throughout.

All their pain and sorrow,
as they cry out across
the world.
It's getting to YOU!

YOU can't take any more.
The cries of injustice,
the jailed throughout
the land.

YOUR people are tired.
Who knows this more
than YOU!

It breaks the heart
of all Heaven
to hear their *boo-hoo's*.
To hear their cries
of injustice,
their cries of shame
and pain.

Their cries of financial ruin
to just name a few.
YOUR people are hurting
and it breaks YOUR heart.

YOU love them without
measure,
in the world throughout.
YOU'LL save them

Prophetic Utterances

once more with
YOUR eternal love
and style.
Breaking all deceptions
and stories of denial.

YOU'LL save them from
the enemies of the land
and put them on
grand stands throughout
the land.

YOU'LL save them with love.
It's the cry of YOUR heart
before YOU send down
YOUR SON with authority
to judge.

YOU'LL save them from
the deceits and lies
of this age,
as YOU prepare in heaven
and set forth YOUR stage.

YOUR stage of elegance
beyond all compare,
as YOU waltz from the heavens
on the clouds of the air.

YOU'LL reign KING SUPREME
in the hearts of YOUR people,
including me.

YOU'LL reign in a heavenly dance,
as YOU *woo in* and *romance*
the ones whom YOU love
in an eternal trance.

YOU'LL show each new step
and twirl and such,
as YOU dance through

The Cry of His Heart

the stars and glide
through the heavens.

YOU'LL love, YOU'LL lead
with great heavenly speed,
dancing and romancing
with YOUR eternal nudge
causing feet to budge
from place to place
taking them across
the place.

YOU'LL dance them to
Heaven with YOUR
eternal charm.
Taking their arm
and twirling them
all around.
Dancing on rooftops,
on heavenly doors,
up walls and ravines,
as YOU dance where
YOU please.

YOU'LL pull them and
place them with YOUR
eternal ease,
picking them off the
floor on bended knee.
YOU'LL wine them
and dine them
from all over the
world.

It is the way
YOU do things with
YOUR heavenly twirl.
YOU'LL glide in every
city, every town
far and wide,

Prophetic Utterances

every village
and hut in the world
throughout.

YOU'LL dance for
miles on end
collecting YOUR loved ones
taking them to a world
without end.

YOU'LL dance in the heavens
and the world down
below as YOU gather
YOUR loved ones—
of which YOU all know.

YOU love them with style,
with great finesse
YOU dress them in
style in a royal dress.

A suit of splendor from
THE LORD OF THE FEAST
as YOU dance them
to YOUR dinner
YOUR glorious feast.

They'll have wine
as cocktails.
The finest wine ever,
for them to taste,
to drink and savor
this *new wine*
from heaven
the one YOUR SON
did make.

We'll drink in HIS love
on this royal date.
We'll have life eternal
with THE KING OF THE DANCE.

The Cry of His Heart

The Romance of Heaven
is beginning to take shape.

The Dance of Heaven
in the shape of a dove,
sent down from Heaven
HIS royal love dove.

The doves will be flying
and circling about,
as THIS KING OF GLORY
finishes off HIS *Earthly Story*
and seals it with a
heavenly kiss.

It's a show you
surely don't want
to miss.
So, *get ready! Prepare!*
Everyone down *there*
The Wedding
is all planned
The Time is at hand
for THE KING OF GLORY
to finish up HIS Story
for love and glory
from story to story.

Zephaniah 3:14-20, Matthew 22:1-14

Prophetic Utterances

PREPARE FOR THE WEDDING

Across the land
for THIS GOD called MAN
and THIS MAN called GOD.
HE is THE GROOMSMAN
coming for HIS love.
*The Chosen Ones
of Israel* from
across the land.
They are in HIS heart
and in HIS hand.
HE loves them
without measure
HE loves them
without end.

They are HIS chosen people
A royal priesthood.
It is HIS Plan since
before the earth began.
To gather them up from
across the land.
To heal them and restore
them.
It's HIS Royal Race—
No more wars and
earthly disgrace.
They'll have joy written
across their face.
They are eternally MINE!

Says, THE MAKER of all things
I'VE wined them and
dined them making
them MY Bride.
I will go on collecting

The Cry of His Heart

them from far and wide.
They will have life eternal
in a world without end.

I'VE chosen them
and crowned them
and made them MY friend.
They'll reign in the heavenlies
and on the earth down below.
I'LL put them in places
where they ought to go.
They are MY CHOSEN,
MY FEW who have
been slaughtered
and beaten and
picked on by man.
I will raise them up
and show forth their
glory in all the land.

I'LL wipe the shame
off their face and
restore their smile
in a while,
as I see them
through yet another
turbulent trial.
They'll have life
ever after, mercy
without end.
They'll have life
everlasting,
mercy without end
with THE ONE
who has chosen them
who is now their friend.

They'll cling to ME as
if I were their mother
for all eternity.

Prophetic Utterances

They'll have life
everlasting,
mercies galore.
They have no idea
just what's in store.
MY love never ends
MY mercies are great.
I came to redeem.
MY way is first rate.
*Nothing is wasted
nothing is lost*
all will be found
when they put on
their gown.
They will reign with
ME
for all eternity.
It is MY plan in
the world throughout
I really am devout
in MY Church
throughout.
And I will come
with *a mighty shout!*

So *The Time* is now,
it's really at hand
to get yourself ready
throughout the land.
Time is a wasting
The Time Clock is
ticking for all to
climb aboard.
Head for the shore
and sail with
ME
for all eternity
forevermore.

Isaiah 61:7, Jeremiah 30:3

The Cry of His Heart

SATAN'S DEMISE

All power and authority
has been given to HIM
to lead forth the charge
on the powers that be.
HE'LL break them
and destroy them,
in the world without
end.
Because they denied HIM,
HE'S not their friend.
HE'LL issue a blast with
HIS heavenly shofar.
They will hear it from
near and from very far.

HIS trumpets are
raising all across
the land
to issue in this
final command
in a world without
measure,
in a world without
end.
HE'LL tidy up the land
and even the score.
HE'LL knock them
off their feet
and they will fall
to the floor.

HE'LL knock them
off their perch and
send them reeling
through the sky.

Prophetic Utterances

It is *the reason*
that HE *chose* to die.
To put an end to
the trouble that brews.
The injustice that abounds,
the trouble ahead
of you.
He's here for a moment
only a moment of time
then for all eternity
he will be MINE!

No more able to plow
MY people under.
He has been made
to wholly surrender.
It's not his style
to be found in a crutch,
to be cast down to
the ground with
only mud to suck.
It's not bad
karma or even
bad luck.
It's his impending
doom which shall
arise.

I'VE taken this too
long!
I'VE HELD MY PEACE!
NOW, it is time
for MY RELEASE!
To show him
he's a loser
and the world
he has lost!

Seated in Heaven
and no longer

The Cry of His Heart

on *the cross*
I Reign Supreme
for all to see.

From shore to shore
with MY earthly score
in MY hands.
I'LL put evil away
with all authority
forevermore,
with bustling
billows from
Heaven galore.
I'LL knock *Satan*
to his knees
and even the
score.
He'll have life
for eternity
in misery.

Shackled and down
facing straight
down.
Justice will be served
by MY *Royal Hand*.
Justice is served
by MY *Royal Command*!
Justice is served
it serves him right!
For putting MY people
in lives of sheer fright!
He'll get what he
has coming to him—
this is for sure!

Not one ounce of
him is pure.
He's crafty, deceitful
a murderous worm

Prophetic Utterances

who meddled in lives,
while he watched
them squirm.
It's *his time*
to be crushed and be
bruised for his
transgressions at large.

While he is hit with
MY royal barge!
It is his fate!
It is what he chose.
His time is at hand
for infecting your nose!
He squirms in his
mire of earthly deceit,
he's the lowest
of low
he's really a
creep!
He creeps in the day
and all through the night
issuing fear and tremendous
fright.

It is his delight
to put out their light
MY chosen, MY treasures
including you.
He desires death
for MY chosen
MY elect from the
start.
Wreaking his fury,
on the world throughout
Now, it's *his time*
to be tossed in the
rubble, the ruin
of all time.

The Cry of His Heart

To reap what's
sown on the
earth below.
He's had the time
of his life
causing despair,
pummeling MY chosen
ones without any care.
His time is at hand.
His time has come.
This prince of darkness
is only just a bum!
He's had his day!

His day is gone!
His bell has gone
off, and it's only
a bong!
He's *the loser of life,
the loser of all time.*
He never was,
a friend of MINE.
He's nobody's friend.
He's nobody's child.
This son of perdition
has gone his
final mile.
There is no light
within him.

Only darkness galore…
He's getting what's
coming to him,
in a little while.
He's *not* stealing
MY show, *nor*
stealing MY title.
He'll be in *Hades*
in a little while.

Prophetic Utterances

Nestled with his
demons of every kind,
wondering why
he wasn't chosen
to dine.

His arrogance knows
no boundary,
his deceit knows
no end.
His throne is dismantled.
He's a spineless one.
The father of lies
that everyone despises.
He's not known for valor
only quick assorted
schemes and well
planned lies.
Where he used
his demons to tell
white lies.

He's no friend of yours
and he's no friend of MINE.
He's the father of no one,
only sheer lies.
His day is at hand.
His time has come
to be struck over
with blood sent from above
from the blood of THE LAMB,
THE LAMB that was slain.

He'll be thrown into
outer darkness as
he's never known,
by the dismantling
of his power and
the dismantling of
his throne.

The Cry of His Heart

He won't know
what hit him
when he receives
his final blow.
He'll go flying
deep down below.

He'll sing songs of
torment way
off key.
He'll scream
shouts of agony
to name just a few.
This Time has been
coming
and nearly at hand.
I'M redeeming
MY children out of
his hand,
his clutches of death
and despair all
around.

He won't know
what hit him,
as he's on his
way down.
MY children
will be free
from his cruel
twists of fate.
His time is coming,
it's a royal date
the king of demise
the king of the dross
is heading for destruction
because of *the cross*!
He will make no one
a mockery ever again.

Prophetic Utterances

Because I came to
save you before it's
his end.
He will not hurt
you ever again,
because *his time*
is coming, being
led by your FRIEND.
So hang on!
Hold tight!
It will be a *good day*
and even a *good night.*
Beauty will come.
Beauty will stay.
The Day is not
far away.

John 8:44, Revelation 20:1-3

The Cry of His Heart

HOLD ON

Hold fast!
You must overcome
and last!
His impasse is about
finished.
Don't let go of MY
staff!
Hold on with all you've got!
Don't ever let go while
you're down below!
Hold on to MY promises
Hold on to MY heart
Hold on to MY love
in the world throughout.

Hold on to MY Light
in this dark world,
while you travel,
until it's time for ME
to lay down MY gavel.
Don't get discouraged,
too weary to move
Get up! Get going!
We aren't going
to lose!
WE win in the end
it's plain to see—

HANG ON! MY LOVED
ONES I'M COMING
FOR THEE!
Don't give up now!
It's almost time
for you to be
with ME

Prophetic Utterances

for all time.
Hold on to MY FATHER
THE FATHER OF LIGHTS
you're in HIS heart
of which HE *truly* delights!

Please! *Don't* let go
of your hope
of heaven!
Hang on to
the hem of MY cloak!
The hem of
MY garment!

This is *no joke!*
Hold on, hold fast!
I need you to
Hold on, I'm coming
at last!
Don't let go of
ME!

I'M coming MY dear one
I'M coming
at last!!
I need you!
I died for you!
Come home to ME
please!

Choose life,
not death:
it's why I died
on the cross.
To save every last
one before they
are lost.
You'll have life
everlasting,
love through and through.

The Cry of His Heart

MY searchlight is on
I'M looking for *the lost.*
Don't let go of this
life.
Hold on at all costs.

Your reward is
without measure
your riches will endure,
because you chose
to live this life as I
have made you pure.
So, *don't* let go
don't let *the tempter*
take you.
His desire is to
deflate and corrupt you,
to hold you hostage in
this *life of mirage.*

He is a phony
full of baloney.
Don't believe
his lies,
his clever disguise.
He can look real good
and even quite chic.
It's only an *illusion*—
he's trying to fool you.
*He wears many hats
of many colors*
trying to show forth
his pompous wonders.
He is a liar at heart
a deceiver from the start.

Sons and daughters
beware!
In the world throughout,
he'll show you glory

Prophetic Utterances

upon glory,
but, it's really, really gory.
His illusion of lies
will be before your eyes!

Don't believe what you see!
Don't believe what they
tell you!
Don't believe all the lies!
I will come *only* from
heaven with *a mighty shout!*
All the earth will hear
it in the world
throughout!

Stay attuned to MY voice
in the days ahead!
What's coming on earth
is *The Day of Dread*
Hold on to MY hand
Hold on to MY heart
Don't let go—

Because there will be
nowhere to go,
no place to hide.
You will be hidden
in ME—just watch
and see.

I will hold you all
with MY strong
delusion.
You'll be safe in MY
hand,
in MY grasp you will
abide, while I walk
you through to *the other side.*

They will think they

The Cry of His Heart

are hallucinating,
when they come for their
attack,
not knowing, you've been
heavenly hijacked!

I HAVE MY WAYS,
I HAVE MY WHYS
just trust in ME
not the enemy's lies.

Times will get heavy
Times will get tough,
but I *assure* you
I'M with you,
because enough is
enough!
Hold on to ME—

Don't let go!
Don't grow faint!
To him who overcomes
it's a royal date.

The Day of Doom and Dread
is not far off.
It's looming overhead
it's lurking in the shadows.

Philippians 3:12-14, James 1:17

Prophetic Utterances

THE DAY OF DOOM AND DREAD

Is looming overhead.
It's lurking in the shadows
of MY mind,
in the shadows of mystery
and uncertainty.
What is this
Day of Doom and Dread?
Impending *doom* and
impending *dread.*
"Whatever is this about, dear LORD?"

It lurks in the shadows
of time.
It lurks in the sublime.
It is a heavenly curse
sent from above
from *The Great Above*
and *The Great Beyond.*

The Day of Doom and Dread
is looming overhead
it's clear.
The Day of Doom and Dread
is here!
It's about to hit our
atmosphere.
The Days of Doom and Dread
are here!

They will arrive before
we disappear.
They loom, they hover
sent by THE GROOM.

To destroy *mothers of pride,*
the *sons of perdition,*

The Cry of His Heart

the *fathers of lies*,
and the *daughters
of division*.

The Days of Doom and Dread
are approaching.
They are nearly overhead
of the ocean.
They loom,
they are lingering
waiting for direction from
THE CONDUCTOR on high
sent from HIS skies.
They loom,
they are fast approaching.
The melody of man
his music is such,
it makes HIM upchuck.

The rhythms are vile,
the pauses defile.
The lyrics are lies
sent to disguise
his subtle lies of
distorted love.
Satan's diversions are
all devised with a plan
to bring confusion
and calamity to the
land.

The Days of Doom and Destruction
are near
hovering just out of our
atmosphere.
Don't believe the
king of lies.
He infuses music
that is not wise.
He takes captive

Prophetic Utterances

their ears and
distorts the sound to
bring people
way, way down.

THE SON will reappear
it's near!
The Days of Doom and Dread
linger here.
Hovering above
for a little while
before projecting down
and killing *denial,*
the rival of life
and all that is good.

THE FATHER HAS ISSUED
A COMMAND:

*"It is the destruction
of every man
in the land,
that chose not to
enter in and laud*
THE HOST OF HEAVEN
HIS MAJESTY from on high.
*It is the reason
they are going to die."*

HE'LL take two from
here and two from
there.
HE'LL begin to do this
everywhere.
HE'LL follow where
THE SPIRIT leads and
take for HIS own
the ones who are
pleased to know HIM
and serve

The Cry of His Heart

THE KING of
The Holy Atmosphere.

HE'LL save all HIS own
at HIS *Throne of Grace*
and all the others
will fall from the
mace,
the vapors and such.

It will be a day
of horrendous bad
luck!
The Day of Doom and Dread is at hand,
it is fast approaching
this land!
You better get out of the way.
You better stay out of sight.
This Day shall be deadly
all over the land.

THE KING
HAS ISSUED A COMMAND:

"*The Day* is at hand
all over the land!"

Come to
THE FATHER
before it's too late!
Come through
THE SON
before it's too late!
The Time is getting late!
The Doom and The Dread
are looming overhead.

Come to THE FATHER
Come through THE SON
Come really fast!
you really must

Prophetic Utterances

run!
Run for your lives!
Before *The Day* draws
near!
And THE FATHER OF GRACE
will no longer be near.
Run for your shelters!
Run for cover!
This Day will be like
no other!

THE FATHER OF TIME
THE FATHER OF MERCY
is coming for all
the bloodthirsty!
HE'LL put them in
their place, showing
all their disgrace.
The Time is at hand
all over the land.
The Days of Doom
and Gloom linger
above.
Sent by OUR FATHER,
THE FATHER OF LOVE.

It is HIS commission;
It is HIS decree
to put an end
to the crimes
on all humanity.

HE'S issued *The Call*
sent out HIS warning—
of what's ahead
for this world throughout.
There is no time to think
and doubt.
The Day is dawning
in the world throughout.

The Cry of His Heart

There will be screaming
and shouting and gnashing
of teeth.
People passing out
from sheer dread.

Overwhelmed by the
sounds of ringing alarms.
Overwhelmed by the smoke
and overcome by
the rubble.
It is *The Day of Trouble*
which is lingering
near.
It is just lingering
and looming above.
Sent by THE FATHER
with love!

To put an end to
the violence on
HIS people through-
out,
until JESUS comes
with a mighty shout!
HE'LL SHOUT with excitement!
HE'LL SHOUT for sheer joy.
HE'LL SHOUT for every
man, woman and
every girl and boy.

It'll be HIS day of victory!
That has been spoken of
in the past.
The *New Day* is dawning.
Finally—and at last!
Prepare! Before it is too
late!

Prophetic Utterances

Get yourself ready
for HIS MAJESTY to take
HIS stand from Heaven
above.
It is a royal command!
The Show's about to start
in the world throughout,
without a doubt!

Proverbs 16:4, Jeremiah 17:17-18

The Cry of His Heart

THE DAWN OF THE MILLENIUM

A *New Day* is dawning
in front of you,
before you,
ahead of you,
bringing you closer to ME.

In MY haven of rest
for *the faithful,*
the true,
the tried and true believers,
of the earth.

No more
wandering around aimlessly,
like scavenger birds.
Wholly beloved,
wholly true.

Psalms 107:29-32, Revelation 19, 21, 22

Prophetic Utterances

HE LOVES WITHOUT END

Those HE calls HIS friend
from here to eternity
without end.
HE doesn't give up on us
wayward ones.
HE doesn't love the
seemingly perfect ones
more.

HE loves us all it's
an even score.
Some take more time
to harness in and tame.
Sometimes, they have
to experience more pain,
but HE loves them the
same.

No pain, no gain!
It's how HE plays
HIS game—
come win, lose
or draw.

HE loves them all
because
HE is
THE FATHER of all.
HE has
a *father's* heart
a *father's* love
a *father's* commitment
a *father's* love for all
a *father's* authority
a *father's* duplicity
a *father's* amazing grace

The Cry of His Heart

how sweet the sound
that saved a wretch like
me!

HE *LOVES* and *LOVES*
and *LOVES*
It is what HE does!
It is HIS style
It is HIS way
THIS MAKER of Heaven
and the great blue skies.

HE *LOVES* without measure
HE *LOVES* without end
HE *LOVES* us all and
calls us HIS friend
HE *LOVES* us for all time
because HE is our
friend.

It is HIS style
it is HIS finesse,
to take what is broken
and really a mess.
To fix what was broken
and nail it to HIS cross.
All is *not* dross and
all is *not* lost.
All is *not* forsaken
it was all for *a cost.*
It cost HIM *Dearly*
It cost HIM *Severely*
HE paid it all in full.

It was our guarantee,
our ransom from on high.
It was why HE sent
HIS SON and allowed
HIM to die.
To save us all from

Prophetic Utterances

impending *doom,*
so we could have
life again,
and be restored soon.
It's a day of gladness
awaiting ahead.

THE MASTER has spoken,
it is the way HE led.
From roof tops and
chimney tops,
HE'LL shout it out loud,
"THIS IS WHY I SENT
MY BELOVED CHILD!!"
To forgive all your sins,
your trespasses and such.

To take you out of
Satan's clutch.
HE loved us that much!

Proverbs 3:12, 1 John 4:7-21

The Cry of His Heart

WHAT LIES AHEAD

Is eternal chatter
exposing the truth
and what was really
the matter.
HE'LL dispel all the lies.
HE'LL expose all the truths.
This is no "eternal spoof!"
It is real!

There's *no* mystery about it.
No cloud to shroud it.
It's eternal truth.
There's *no* doubt about it.
The Time is at hand.
Will you jump aboard
to meet your LORD?

THE MASTER of *The Heavens,*
THE MASTER of *The Seas*
desires your presence
at HIS royal knees.
You'll bow before HIM
worship and adore
HIM.
HE is THE KING OF KINGS
THE LORD OF MAJESTY
and all things.
HE'S THE LORD of all,
and *all* won't you
please?

HE'LL usher a toast
with joy in HIS heart
in the world throughout.
HE'LL say with a shout,
"I LOVE MY CHILDREN

Prophetic Utterances

IN THE WORLD THROUGHOUT!"
HE'S really quite devout
THIS MAN from on high
who was sent from
heaven to make the way
for you and I.

HE'LL sail from the heavens
and through the atmosphere,
it's getting close and
oh, so near!

The excitement is growing
from within HIS heart
to sail from the heavens
in the world throughout.
HIS Time is at hand
throughout all the land.
HE'LL usher a blow
on the earth down below
and bring in a dance
with *royal romance,*
with *majestic style.*
There will be no more
denial
no cheating style.
It'll happen soon,
in a very short while.
So get yourselves ready!
Get yourselves all prepared.

I'M Coming quite soon!
Says, THE GROOM.
MY Time is at hand.
MY Time now is short.
MY Time will surely
not abort.
It is on schedule.
It is on time
to take what is MINE,

The Cry of His Heart

for forever and all time!
The Time is getting late.
The time is getting short.
Get ready! Get set!
You haven't much time
left.

HE'LL shout from
the heavens.
HE'LL shout through
the lands
making well known
all of HIS plans.

HE reigns KING ETERNAL
THE GOD from on high.
It is why HE sent
HIS SON to die.
Get ready! Get set!
The Ship has already
set sail.
HE'S setting
you free and out
of *this jail*—
no time is left.

Says, THE ETERNAL CHEF
Get ready! Get set!
I AM on MY jet!
Getting ready to land
and take over MY land
for every girl and boy
and every woman
and man.

MY Time is about here.
MY Time has come,
to take out
MY royal gun
for *evil* to shun!

Prophetic Utterances

I'LL shut its mouth,
its lips I'LL split—
and bring out
MY royal *whip*!
I'LL *whip* it clean
I'LL *whip* it long
I'LL *whip* it wide
and I'LL *whip* it strong.

I'LL *whip* it once
I'LL *whip* it twice
one for *The Show*
and one for the dice.
I'LL *whip* with MY
everlasting style.
I'LL *whip* it away—
this gruesome decay.
I'LL *whip* it away,
for it surely can't stay!
I'LL *whip* from MY heavens
I'LL *whip* from MY skies,
this king of demise
and all kinds of lies.
I'LL show him *WHO'S
BOSS*!
I'LL show him
WHO wins!
I'LL show him
MY CROSS!
I'LL show him
his loss!
*I won that day
on the cross!*

Now, it's time to come
and pick up MY *lost*,
MY *battered* and *bruised*,
MY *chosen*, MY *few*
who will reign with

The Cry of His Heart

ME forever and ever
in *a new* with
amazing sand,
and glorious sights,
with all its delights.
It's awesome!
It's wonderful!
It's an amazing sight!
Sparkles galore,
reigns of majesty,
royal chariots
of fire
that never retire.
Floating chariots
and floating boats
that can't sink!
Freighters galore
and streaming
shores.

ONE for the heavens
ONE for the show
ONE for HIS glory
ONE for HIS story
ONE for THE FATHER
ONE for THE SON
ONE for eternity
that has already
WON!
ONE for the captain
ONE for the chaplain
ONE for the laymen
ONE for the day men
ONE for the doctor
ONE for the mayor
ONE for THE FATHER
ONE for the DOVE
ONE for the money
ONE for the show

Prophetic Utterances

ONE ought to *get set*
in the world down below.
ONE for all and all
for ONE.

Mark 1:15, Revelation 22:1-21

The Cry of His Heart

THE KING OF THE HEAVENS

THE KING of *The Show*
is getting ready to reign
on the earth down below.

HE'LL REIGN in HIS style
HE'LL REIGN in HIS cross
HE'LL REIGN in victory
and count it not lost.
HE'LL REIGN in HIS lost ones
HE'LL REIGN from on high
HE'LL REIGN with HIS love
from heaven above.

It is HIS HEART
It is HIS WAY
It is HIS DAY
to usher in HIS PRESIDENCY.
No longer a candidacy
The Victory's been won!
HE'S the declared winner!
from heaven above.

Will you come for
HIS dinner?
Will you come for
new wine?
Will you come for
the entertainment
and dine?
Will you come
for THE FATHER?
Will you come
for THE SON?
Will you come
for the last time?

Prophetic Utterances

And just watch
HIM shine?

HE'LL *shine* with a radiance
of love
HE'LL *shine* from the heavens
in pure solid love
HE'LL *shine* in magnificence
HE'LL *shine* in sheer splendor
HE'LL *shine* from the heavens
forever and ever.

HE'LL *outshine* the sun
HE'LL *outshine* all shame
HE'LL *outshine* all misery
and *outshine* all blame
HE'LL *outshine* all sinners
and all eternally lost
HE'LL *outshine* the ones
who denied HIS Cross
HE'LL *outshine* it all
as HE reigns from on high
HE'LL *outshine* the heavens
and all the dross
HE'LL *outshine*
HIS everything and
everybody's neighbor.

HE'LL shine with great
excellence
with exuberant style
HE'LL shine with an
everlasting smile
HE'LL glow
HE'LL radiate
for all to see
HE'LL glow with great
glory
for all the world to see.
HE'LL glow as HE tells

The Cry of His Heart

HIS Story—
It's time to close now,
it's time to stop.
I'VE shared MY heart
with the world throughout.

John 8:12, Revelation 21:22-25

Prophetic Utterances

I WAS UNAWARE OF HIS PRESENCE

I felt the emptiness abound.
I felt panicky and clingy
like a grasping child
"Don't go! Don't leave me!"
I grasped at HIS words
I rubbed my fingers
through them.
My eyes welled up
and my heart sank.
Oh, how I'll miss
HIM if HE'S done
writing through me!
I need HIM *now* more
than ever.

"Fear not, MY child!"
I just heard HIM say,
I'M in your heart
forever I'LL stay.
I'LL never leave you or
forsake you
this is for sure.

I love you for now and
forever in a day.
MY love is everlasting
MY love endures
MY love is sure and
MY love is pure
MY love outshines
darkness and sadness
and such.

MY love knows no end.
MY love is all that matters.
I love you without measure

The Cry of His Heart

I love you for all time
I love you—it's what I do
for you.
Nothing can separate you
from this love of MINE!
I will love you forever
and love you for all time.
Don't get all worried.
Don't get all sad.
I will love you for always,
just like MY DAD!

WE love you the same.
WE aren't playing a game
with your heart.
WE aren't wanting
to hurt you like
those of your past.
Like their love that
did not last.
WE love you—forever,
and *OUR LOVE* will last!
It's time to get ready
to start your day
OUR writing is now
ending—
make the most
of your day.

OUR writing is not finished.
OUR writing is not done.
It's time to take a break
and go have some fun.
I love you, dear child
I love you for sure
I won't walk away
from you.
I'LL walk beside you
every step of the way.

Prophetic Utterances

I'LL live inside of you,
forever I will stay.
I won't leave your side.
I'LL *never* desert you.
You are the apple of
MY eye.

MY love is unending
MY love knows no end.
MY love is for sure,
because you are
MY friend.
Rise up, get dressed
you're quite a mess
with tear stained eyes,
and dog licks on your thighs.
Look to the heavens
Look within your heart.
I'M with you
today and forever
without end!

John 17:10-26, Hebrews 13:5-6

The Cry of His Heart

THE KING OF WONDER

HE is THE KING OF WONDER
and THE KING OF GLORY
THE AWESOME and
MAJESTIC ONE
whose story this is!
HE writes upon your hearts
HE writes upon your
hands.

HE is an AMAZING GOD
who once was a MAN.
HE came for all eternity
HE came for you and me.
It's why HE came to
the cross
for you and for me.

It is THE KING OF GLORY'S
STORY
it is HIS MASTERPIECE.
The stains upon
HIS hands and knees
were implemented
piece by piece.

HE is THE KING OF WONDER
THE KING of you and I.
It is *the reason*
HE *chose* to die
for the likes of
you and I.

We'll have eternity
forevermore.
No more sorrow
and *no more* shame.

Prophetic Utterances

It's *the heavenly score*
from shore to shore
way beyond measure
and so much more.

HE'LL ride through
the heavens
HE'LL ride through the sky
HE'LL radiate from heaven.
It's a royal date!
HE'LL beam with a
brilliance for all the
world to see
and fly through
the sky for
you and I.

This awesome
KING OF WONDER
The TRULY MAJESTIC ONE
The TRUE and FAITHFUL ONE
HIS CHOSEN and
BELOVED SON
HE is THE HOLY ONE.

Psalms 68:4, Matthew 3:17

The Cry of His Heart

YOU LOVE US SO MUCH

That YOU chose to
die.
Eliminating an eye for
an eye
a tooth for a tooth.

YOUR Plan is designed
in a fashion from
above.
It is *the reason*
YOU chose us to
love.

YOU love us without
measure.
YOU love us for all
time.
It is *the reason*
we've been invited to
dine.

YOU welcome us all
YOU'VE invited us
here
to show us
YOUR wonders
which are really quite
near.

YOU are in a sphere
of celestial proportions
that are giant proportions
of eternity strong.

Prophetic Utterances

YOU love us all day
and all through the
night.

YOUR mercy knows no
end.
YOUR valor is
YOUR poignant truth.

YOU speak *LOVE*
all over the
Earth.

YOU spell *LOVE*
by YOUR eternity
standards.

YOU make *LOVE*
with melody in
me.

YOU are *LOVE*—
YOUR MAJESTY!
YOU make rhyme
with no reason
and reason with no
rhyme.

YOU are majestic
and sure.
YOU'RE really quite
divine.

YOU love rhyme
with reason
and reason with
love
sent by THE FATHER
on the wings of a
dove.

The Cry of His Heart

YOU spell *natural
disaster*
YOUR splendid
way.

YOU shake the heavens
above
with YOUR amazing
love.
YOU love with all
zeal
from eternity
strong.

LOVE from THE MASTER
from the world up
above.
LOVE from THE FATHER
LOVE from THE SON
LOVE from the
Heavenlies
LOVE from above.

LOVE from THE MASTER
of heaven above
LOVE for all measure
LOVE for all time.

LOVE in the meaningless
LOVE in the wine
LOVE in the earth
beneath
LOVE without
measure.

LOVE never rests
LOVE never stops
LOVE never quits
LOVE never ceases
or ever desists.

Prophetic Utterances

LOVE is everlasting
LOVE is right on time
LOVE is hovering over us
in the sublime.

YOUR love is eternal
YOUR love is sheer grace.

YOUR love is never-
ending
on the human race.
YOU love like no other
YOU love like a mother
and love like THE FATHER
of all time.

Psalms 37:28, 1 John 4:7-21

The Cry of His Heart

YOU ARE THE KING ETERNAL

THE KING of all time
YOU are THE ONE
who invited us to
dine.

Come to *The Party*
come for *The Show*
three to get ready
and four to go.

One for eternity
one for all time
one for HIS MAJESTY
one for new wine.

One for all purpose
one for all time
one for each one of
us
one for all time.

HE is THE KING OF FLAVOR
sent from above.
Sending HIS love to
flavor us with love
from above.

HE is THE KING OF ETERNAL GUISE
HE is THE KING ETERNAL
THE KING is quite wise!

HE moves with melody
the melody of love
sent from THE FATHER OF LOVE.

It is about *time* to finish
up HIS Story

Prophetic Utterances

for THE KING of all glory
and glory and glory.

It's time to stop,
but not time to
finish.
No matter the time
we will surely finish.

One for all time
one for all eternity
one for the love of GOD
for all eternity at
large.

One for the measure
one for the show
three to get ready
and four to go.

HE'LL reign from
the heavens
straight from the
sky.

HE'LL reign in majestic
majesty from
on high.

It is *the reason*
HE *chose to* die
HE'LL reign in eternity
HE'LL reign from the skies.
We are *the ones* HE seeks
both you and I.

HE loves us from ever after
from *The Great Unknown*
HE loves from above
straight from HIS Throne.

The Cry of His Heart

HE loves us for all Eternity
HE loves us for all time
HE loves, that's what HE
does!

Psalms 24:7-10, 47:8, 146:10; Micah 4:1-5

Prophetic Utterances

OUR GOD ETERNAL

When reading
A poem of compassion
a poem of all love
a poem of endearing
great love.

A poem for all treasure
a poem for all time
a poem from OUR
FATHER above.

HE operates in poetry
HE operates that in me
HE operates the universe
and every single verse.

HE operates in majesty
HE operates in you
and me.

HE operates in harmony
HE operates in majesty
HE operates for the world
to see.
HE operates in you and me

HE maneuvers o*ur race*
with amazing grace.
HE maneuvers our existence
HE goes the distance
HE'S never out maneuvered
HE'S never outdone.

Because our GOD ETERNAL
is number one.
HE'LL lead with HIS charge

The Cry of His Heart

for all the world to
see.

HE'LL lead us all to
victory!
HE'LL lead with HIS style
HE'LL lead with HIS fashion
HE'LL lead
The War of Eternity
HE'S really *combatin'*

HE leads, HE guides
HE walks beside
HE leads with HIS
eternity fashion
HE leads *the combatin'*
HE leads with an
eternal stride
HE leads—it's how
HE spells *action!*

HE leads, HE guides
HE walks beside
HE leads without
injustice.
HE leads every score
HE guides far and wide
with an eternal stride
HE guides without
end.

HE guides in HIS own
fashion
HE guides us down
and in between
HE guides for all
eternity.

HE guides for good
measure

Prophetic Utterances

HE guides for good
show
HE guides for full
measure
which way we
should go.

HE is *Our Eternal Guide*
Our Eternal Stride
HE leads the heavens
and the earth beneath.

HE leads all of heaven
at *the stroke of eleven.*

HE leads with all heaven
HE leads for all time.
It's why you've been
invited to wine and
to dine!

Psalms 23, Isaiah 48:17

The Cry of His Heart

THE HOST OF HOSTS

HE'LL raise HIS glass
as HE ushers in *a toast*
to all of those who did
the most
for THE KING and for
THE HOST
who hosted our existence.

HE'S THE HOST OF HOSTS
HE throws quite
a party
quite a party post-
host.
A party of gladness
no sadness allowed
only joy and great
gladness in
the world through-
out.

There really is no
question.
There really is no doubt.
HE'S THE HOST with the
most to host about!

HE'LL host in the heavens.
HE'LL host in the seas.
HE'LL host those on
bended knees.

HE'LL host from on
high
HE'LL host this side
of heaven
before it strikes

Prophetic Utterances

eleven.
HE'LL host in heaven
with *royal divine
leaven.*

HE'LL raise the score
and do much more
to salute THE KING
for HIS Eternal War,
HE'LL salute
THE SAVIOR
of you and me
HE'LL salute HIS
veterans from
overseas.

HE'LL salute,
not rebuke the choices
we've made.
It'll be fine wine and
a royal parade,
parading all our acts
of obedience and
service.

Our lifelong eternal
eternity of service.
HE'LL lead for all
measure
HE'LL lead for all
time.

It's *the reason*
you've been
invited to dine!

One for the money
One for the show
three to get ready
and *four* to go.

The Cry of His Heart

Go from your homes
your churches below
Go from the cities
for mile after mile.

Go to the city
Go to the park
Go to THE SAVIOR
before it gets dark!

Go while you've got
time
Go while you still
can
Go for THE SAVIOR
The once called Man.

Go for eternity
Go for no end
Go for THE ONE
who is *our Friend.*

Go to THE GOD
who leads with poetic
grace.
Go to THE GOD
of the human race.

Go for the money
of eternal time.
Go for the show
on the earth below.

Go forever
forever without
end.
Go for OUR SAVIOR
our ETERNAL FRIEND.
HE is THE KING
OF JUSTICE.
HE is THE KING OF GRACE.

Prophetic Utterances

HE is THE KING OF WONDER
of *The Eternal Race.*

Shoot from your wallet
Shoot for the stars
Shoot for the heavens
you eternal jars.

Shoot for all heavens
Shoot for the stars
aim for the heavens and
aim for HIS face.

HE is THE FATHER OF LOVE
THE FATHER OF GRACE
THE FATHER OF MERCY
THE FATHER OF THE STARS
THE FATHER OF ALL LIGHTS.
So set your sights
on Heaven
set your sights on
earth.

Psalms 84:12, Isaiah 43:11

The Cry of His Heart

HEED MY WARNING CRY

Get yourself ready!
For this brand new birth,
as HE sails from the heavens
to the earth beneath.

Put oil in your lamps
keep them burning
Put oil in your lamps
keep them burning.

Put oil in your lamps
keep them stirring
Put oil in your lamps.

IT'S A WARNING!!!

Put oil in your lamps
while you can
Put oil in your lamps
all you in the land
Put oil in your lamps
while you still can!

HEED MY WARNING!
HEED MY CALL!
HEED MY VOICE!
One and all!

Heed together
Heed apart
Heed before
"the stampede"
begins to start!

Prophetic Utterances

It is MY WARNING
CRY!
It is MY HEART
to save salvation
with a brand new
start.

Heed MY CALL
one and all
The Show's about
to start on the
world throughout.

TIME is at hand
Time is at heart
Time is running out
in the world through-
out.

TIME is at *the gates*
it's getting real
late.
Time will travel
Time will never
be late.
Time is an energy
from THE FATHER of all eternity
and
THE FATHER of all time
Time is getting
closer.

It's hovering above
THE TIME to act is
Now!
The Time to plan
is today!
The Time to meet
YOUR MAKER
isn't far away!

The Cry of His Heart

Come for the money
Come for the show
three to get ready
and four to go.

Go to your altars
Go to your elders
Go to your pastors
Go to your priests
Go to your mayor

Go to the heavens
reach for the stars
there's not much
time left
for these clay jars!

TIME is at hand
all over the land
Time is nearly finished
Time will be diminished.

TIME will not wait
Time will not stop
Time will continue.

TIME will wind down
Time will tick away
without a doubt.

You've heard MY COMMAND
all across the land
step into your stations!

Rise to the occasion!
It's no time to be lazin'
or lurking about.
Time is about to
run out!

Prophetic Utterances

You've heard MY COMMAND
you've heard MY DECREE
you've heard MY HEART
for you and for ME.

I love you with
an everlasting love
I love you for all
time.

Please accept MY OFFER
to wine and to dine
with MY SON
and I.

WE'LL usher in
a *New Day*
A new fresh start
A new beginning
in the world through-
out.

It is OUR passion
It is OUR love
sent from THE FATHER
from above.

I'VE sent out *This Warning*
I'VE sent it with love
I'VE sent it with
kingly style from
up above.

Now, hear MY CALL
One and all!
Answer your
COMMANDER IN
CHIEF!

CHIEF OF THE ARMIES
CHIEF OF THE HOSTS

The Cry of His Heart

CHIEF OF THE WORLD above
CHIEF OF THE MOST

With HIS chiefly style
HIS renowned ability
HE saves civility
before it's too late!

It's starting to get
ready
It's starting to take shape
It's starting to start
in the world throughout.

Get to your stations!
Get to your stores!
Get to your grocers
before there is no more!

Get in place
where I will send
you!

I'll take you there
mile by mile.
It's going to be a trial
The Trial of all trials!
Says, YOUR COMMANDER
Says, YOUR CHIEF.

Run for the money
Run for the show
three to get ready
four to go.

I had to raise MY Warning
I had to raise MY Flag
TIME is getting out of hand
all over the land.

Proverb 12:15, Matthew 25:1-13

Prophetic Utterances

IT'S THE ELEVENTH HOUR

No parking
on *The Jersey Shore*
No parking anymore.
No stalling around
it's getting late
No parking
it's too late!

It's no time for
pleasure
and fussing about.
It's time to get ready
for YOUR SAVIOR
to meet.

No time to go to
distant shores.
The Time is now!
What path will
you take?

There's no time to
placate.
No time to daydream
No time to fool around
it's getting late.

Head for THE MASTER'S
Shore.
HIS shore of *Liberty*
really sets you
free for all eternity.

Head for the markets
head for the stores
there is fruit

The Cry of His Heart

just *a waitin'*
to be picked.
They're really ripe
to ripe to sit.
*"Get them on
The Battleship!"*

THE WAR of *The Heavens*
THE WAR of *The Oceans*
THE WAR of *The Chosen*
in the world through-
out.

Is right upon us
it's coming up fast.
The Sail is half-mast
and ready to drift.

It'll drift through
the mornings
It'll drift through
the night
It'll drift through
the heavens.

It'll drift through
the open shores
It'll drift through
the heavens
It's *The Eleventh Hour*
get ready to board
ship!

I'LL meet you and
guide you
every step of the way
taking captivity away.

I'LL take for MY OWN
those far from home
and set them on a

Prophetic Utterances

solid rock
MY Throne.

I'LL take captivity lost
and survivors at sea
delivering them
to MY CROSS.
It's where we
meet.

I'LL take them
MY WAY
not just down
any highway
of eternity dross
I'LL take them
by way of
the cross.

It's for *the lost*
the ones in despair.
There are many
out there
to just leave all alone
without any care.

I have made a
Declaration of War!
WAR from *The Heavens*
WAR from *On High*
I'VE commissioned you
for something big!
Don't ask why!
It's a royal date
I have with you.

The end draws near
like the rising sun
the setting moon
the distant sky.

The Cry of His Heart

The end draws near
it's time to run!
Run for the highways!
Head for the hills!
Before disaster spills
all over the land.

The end draws near.
It's a command
commissioned all over
the land!

Matthew 24:3-51, 1 John 2:18

Prophetic Utterances

THE ARTIST

HE fills in all the cracks
in my canvas
with HIS beautiful light
adding texture and color
like no other.

HE schemefully plans
every shade of me,
from the cracks
in my canvas
to my whole being.

HE loves to draw
HE loves to paint
HE loves every landscape
and every great lake.
HE loves to pause and
soak it all in.

HE loves the ocean
and HE loves to swim
in the deep blue oceans
to the deep blue seas
HE loves to canvas
HIS place.
HE loves
HIS human race.

HE loves to paint with
dexterity and style
sometimes smooth and
sometimes wild.

HE loves with HIS
artistic touch.

The Cry of His Heart

HE loves, HE loves
HE loves so much!

HE loves to bring beauty
into the world.
HE loves and HE loves
out of this world.
HE simplistically paints
and easily draws
either mountains
or four little paws.

HE loves to paint
HE loves to draw
HE loves most
of all.

Watch as THE ARTIST
shines tonight.
HIS every move
is such a delight.
HE moves, HE draws
and so much more
and one day
HE'LL even *the score*.

HE moves with simplicity
HE moves with grace
HE moves mountains
before us
and *Hell* beneath us.

HE lives, HE draws
HE needs an applause
HE needs an ovation
all over HIS play station.

HE moves with all ease
not aiming to please.

Prophetic Utterances

HE sends believers
to their knees.

HE ushers in a mighty blow
from heaven above
to the earth below.

HIS Plan is dramatic
HIS style is real wild
HIS taste is first rate
on HIS royal date
not wishing to please
or caring what's the
matter.

Job 26:7-14, Proverbs 8:27-30

The Cry of His Heart

THE MAD HATTER

HE is THE MAD HATTER
OF HEAVEN
HIS ROYAL MAJESTY
HE'S designed to
save humanity
from
destruction himself.

HIS Plan is quite stealth
with HIS royal wealth
knocking sin on the
floor
and off its shelf
blowing away all despair
with HIS holy air.

HE'LL diminish
and finish
The Greatest Story
of all time.

Without any reason
without any rhyme
HE'LL knock off crime
and wretched decree
sent against you
and ME.

HE'LL free us from slavery
HE'LL set us free.
It is HIS royal decree
to save what is lost
and what has been
stolen
and purchase the cost
with CHRIST ON THE CROSS.

Prophetic Utterances

HE'LL aim it
HE'LL frame it
HE'LL set it in a kiln
HE'LL take control of it
while HE finishes
HIS film.
Recorded in heaven
Recorded for all time
the major offences
and his assorted crimes.
He'll eat from the cinders.
He'll eat from the grave.
This one called Satan
who made you a slave.

HE'LL put slavery
in its place
HE'LL put mockery
out of its pace
and shoot forth from
heaven with all
sorts of leaven.

HE'LL free us from
our past
HE'LL save us with
HIS truth
HE'LL deliver us
from slavery and misery
and disasters and such.

HE is THE KING OF GLORY
and this is
HIS majestic story.
Sent from above
in the shape of love.

Love for all time
Love for eternity long
Love for *the season*

The Cry of His Heart

Love for *the dawn.*
It is *the reason*
HE *chose to die*
because of HIS GREAT love
for you and I.

So, take from
the eternal sink
suck it in and savor
before you swallow.
Drink from the heavens
Drink from MY cup
Drink before
it's time to
upchuck!

Time is a wasting
Time is at hand
Time goes before us
all over the land.

Time is for all
eternity long
for *the brave*
and *the strong*
who avoid all
the wrong.

Hear the *ding dong*
Hear the bell
Hear the warning bell
sounding the alarm.

Get Ready!
Get into your place!
HIS *Time* is at hand
to spray HIS mace.

HE'LL seek HIS thunder
from the grandstand
on high

Prophetic Utterances

HE'LL seek HIS lightning
from above the sky
HE'LL seek HIS virtue
from Heaven above
HE'LL seek HIS promise
it is all around us.

HE'LL seek before
it is too late
and there be
no escape.
HE'LL seek from heaven
and the deep blue
skies
the hurting hearts
and all their cries.

HE hears them
from heaven
HE hears them
from HIS Throne
they are never
alone.

Psalms 147:3-6, James 4:7-10

The Cry of His Heart

DRIVING INTO THE SUN

Is not easy—
Driving into the Sun
is no easy task
with the way before you
in clouded light.
It makes seeing
seem way out of sight.

Driving in the Sun
we'll be home
at last!

Driving into the sun
is no easy task.
It can be painful
and difficult
to see through your
glass windows
before you—
and you can't see
what's ahead
of you.

The Sun magnifies
the debris on the
glass.

Driving into eternity
is *not* for the *faint-hearted*
or the *easily distracted*
to name just a few.

Driving into eternity.
Driving into space
is led by
The Spirit of Grace.

Prophetic Utterances

Grace for the passenger
Grace for the driver
Grace down the hill
and up the other.

Grace of all style
Grace of all love is
Grace for forgiveness
coming from the sky.

Grace of forgiveness
Grace from above
Grace from THE FATHER above.

Love before grace
Love for good measure
Love for eternity
led by grace
Grace leads the way
for sinners like you.

Love for good measure
Love for good score
Love for all time
eternity and more.

John 1:17, Ephesians 2:8-10

The Cry of His Heart

THE KING OF THE UNIVERSE

HE has schemes and
HE has style
wiping away all of denial.

HE'S first rate!
THE KING of the landscape
and the role that HE
takes.

Forever on time
Forever above
Forever walking
in love.

THE KING OF THE UNIVERSE
THE KING indeed
is in search of you
and me.

HE leads with a style
all HIS own
from *The Throne*
of Heaven.

It's almost eleven!
The eleventh hour
will be here in an
hour.

From
the watchtower
from on high

Prophetic Utterances

HE flies from above
in the shape of *LOVE*
showing HIS dignity.

Psalms 45:6, 68:4; Lamentations 5:19

The Cry of His Heart

THE FINAL JEOPARDY

Study ME like jeopardy
every category that refers
to ME.

I'LL ask you a question
you tell ME why?

You only get one try
before you die.

You'll be racing
against *time.*

You'll be risking
it all.

At *the final jeopardy
study* all categories.

Study all kinds
Study real long.

Before the final
bell goes off.

How much will
you risk?

In *the jeopardy
of all time?*

There is only
one winner
in MY Show.

There will be
all kinds of matches
below.

Prophetic Utterances

It's *the final jeopardy*
for you and for ME.

Matthew 7:7-12, Colossians 1:10-12

The Cry of His Heart

THERE'S BEEN A CHANGE IN TIME

In this world of MINE
A change in season
A change in rhyme
A change in this
heart of MINE.

When the waves
of the world
come crashing down on you,
I'LL carry you
through the storms
of this life.

They're washing over you
the waves of commotion
are rising against you
trying to divide you.
I'LL see you through
the division and such.

The sounds of *division*
are rising up.
The coming division of the land.
Division is rising up.
Its forces are saddling
up.

Proverbs 18:10, Mark 3:25

Prophetic Utterances

DON'T TOUCH THAT DIAL

Don't touch that dial
Don't change the station.
It's a *"wake-up"* call
all over the nation.
Join *The Battalion!*
Join *The Fight!*
THE WAR wages on
from day until night.

Hold on fast!
Hold on strong!
Hold on! Hold on!
Hold on! All the time!

Don't touch that dial
Don't change that station.
It's a *"wake up"* call
all over the nation.

1 Thessalonians 5:16-24, Revelation 3:10-13

The Cry of His Heart

WRITING ALL THESE RHYMES

Are a treasure to
my heart.
As HE pours them
through my soul,
my eyes fill with tears
of joy.

I smile, as I enjoy
HIS style of writing
HIS amazing grace
it touches my soul.

Amazing grace
how sweet the sound
WHO saved a wretch
like me.

It's *no* rebound
it's *no* turn-a-round.
The flood is coming
to town and to shore
and there is way, way
more.

HE makes melody
with my heart,
preparing me for a
fresh new start.

HIS keys are in search
of me.
HIS tempo is sheer
divine.
HE is never out of line
with HIS Plan inside
my mind.

Prophetic Utterances

HE'S preparing quite
a discourse
for all those who are
off course,
to bring them home
where they belong
with *no more* sorrow
no more tears
within HIS heavenly
atmospheres.

HE does it for *LOVE*.
HE does it for measure.
HE does it for score
to make sure
what was lost
comes running through
HIS door.

It's HIS *heavenly score*
and much, much more,
to bring sin to the ground
in a heap and a mound.
To save what was lost
and now what has
been found.

HE'LL sing from
HIS heavenly palace
HE'LL sing from above.
HE'LL sing with HIS chalice
upon HIS palace.

Wiping away all malice.
It won't come near
HIS palace
Like what's on "Dallas."

There's no room
for it here.

The Cry of His Heart

No fornicating style
No unleashed denial
that is totally *not* HIS style.

THE KING OF THE MILE
rides through the heavens
to the earth beneath.

THE COMMANDER IN CHIEF
THE COMMITTED ONE
from above
came to spark *war* and
even up the score.
It won't be fun
it won't be for pleasure.

It'll be for forever
in eternity and more.
It'll be for HIS love
of the human race.

Because what HE sees
is a total disgrace.
A disgrace from HIS honor
and HIS majesty.

HE need *not* bend
the bended knee.
HE need *not* wound
the wounded one.
HE need *not* roust
those who are awake.

HE need *not* stir them up
to sit up straight.
They are already at
the starting gate.

They are *ready* to start
in the world throughout.
They are *ready* to go

Prophetic Utterances

down below.
Ready to heist up
the flag,
it's *no* brag.

To be *ready* to start,
in the world throughout
Ready to run
Ready to stand
all over this land.

They *won't* be outdone
They *won't* be overcome
They are the winners
of eternity
and much, much more.
They'll *reign* in heaven
They'll *reign* from
HIS Throne
They'll *reign* from
on high
They'll never die.

They'll *win The Show*
on the earth below
issuing *a blow*
in HIS royal snow.
They'll stand on their
feet
They'll stand for all
time
These are MY precious ones
They're *ready* to go.

They are *ready* to start
three to get ready
four to go!

They *aren't* timid or
scared
They *are* bold as

The Cry of His Heart

can be
They *are* the chosen ones
sent down below
for *this mighty show.*

They'll *issue a blow*
on the earth below.
They *are* stealing
The Show
with *no* warning
or know.
They *are* commissioned
from on high
to the earth below.
They'll *come* from close
and far away.
HE'LL search the heavens
to find HIS new stars.
HIS ways are majestic
HIS style is real mild
HIS touch is quite grand
HE'S no *ordinary man.*

Sent by THE FATHER with love
to the hurting down *beneath.*
Beneath the stars
Beneath in depravity
underneath it all.

HIS melody of love
HE'S making with me
It is HIS own style
It is HIS own force,
to finish HIS own
discourse
with final force.

It's HIS final main course
all through the land
all through the world.

Prophetic Utterances

It's HIS grand tour
before HE takes
HIS stand!

All will applause
HIS bravery
HE is *One of Three*
for all to see.

One for the money
Two for the show
Three to get ready
Four to go!

Go for the luxury
Go for the grace
Go for the human race

Before I spray *mace*
to really blind them,
to make them lost
for denying *the cross*—
counting it all for loss.

I *didn't* do it for money
I *didn't* do it to show off
I *did* it to save
MY Children
at all cost.

I *did it* for *LOVE*
I *did it* for style
to cut off all lying lips,
as eternity all drips.

It drips and it oozes.
After a while,
it's beginning to
stockpile.
All over the land

The Cry of His Heart

All over the world,
in us throughout.

Will you come for
THE KING of ETERNAL CLOUT?
HE'LL clout HIS way
from Heaven away.
HE'S here to stay
so *do not* delay!

HE'LL run for the money
HE'LL run for the show
HE'LL run for HIS Children
from down below.

HE'LL issue a blow!
They *won't* know what
hit them!
While HE'S preparing
the world to
come down to
get them.
HE'LL show up
with force and grace.

HE'LL tell them what's up!
One for the lost
Two for the few
Three to get ready
Four to start new
HE'LL start one at a time
for all time.
HE'LL start through you
HE'LL parade you around,
like you are a clown.
Making you more than
something to be laughed at,
something to poke fun of.
HE'LL show you HIS

Prophetic Utterances

grace and forgiveness,
and love from beyond.

HE'LL take you for measure
HE'LL take you for good score
HE'LL take you and remake you
through Heaven and
much, much more.

HE'LL take you with *LOVE*
across the land,
as you tell HIS Story.
which is for real.

HE'LL ride with you
in eternity.
HE'LL ride with your
face,
removing all the decay
and debris from
your face.

HE'LL wine you and
dine you,
on HIS majestic floor.
HE'LL escort you
to ribbons galore and
to way, way, much more!
Evening the score
of your deplore.
They deplore you
the ones not from
THE SON.

They *hate* you
so much
they just want to
upchuck.
They *hate* you with style
They *hate* you to your face

The Cry of His Heart

They *hate* you, they *hate* you,
to them, you're such a disgrace.

The disgrace from on high,
to the grace down below,
to the grace down under,
while HE dishes out *a blow*.

No more to be laughed at
No more to concede.
This is why HE chose
to die.
This is why HE bleeds.
HE bled to stop
injustice.
HE *bled* to stop
HIS Children,
by bending them
to their knees.

HE *bled* to stop
injustice to HIS stars,
by bringing them to
their knees.

They've *caused* them
much pain.
They've *caused* them
much shame.
They've *caused* them
much drain,
on the earth down below.

They've *used* there
maneuvers.
They've *used* their class
to poke at MY loved ones.
They really have *no* class
or any true style.
They sit in denial

Prophetic Utterances

for quite a while.
They sit in *The Show*
to muster up their strength
and issue a blow.
A *blow* from down beneath
A *blow* from down below
A *blow* to the face
bringing you shame and
disgrace
all over the place.

Placing you in places,
you ought *not* to go.
Placing you about face
Placing you downward,
while pointing their
gun at you.
and threatening you
to make you stop.
They want you to quit,
to bail ship!
To abandon *Your Call.*

Come to the heavenlies
Come one and come all.
It's *not* dull
It's *not* drab
It's truly exciting,
for one and for all.

Don't ever let them
make you fear,
and then quit.
Don't abandon *Your Call*
Don't quit
The Race!

You'll come out on top
You'll take the lead

The Cry of His Heart

You'll take eternity
without a reed.

A *reed* for good pleasure
A *reed* for good score
A *reed* for much, much more.

HE'LL *reed* in disasters
HE'LL *reed* just for fun
HE'LL *reed* you all in
to eternity to finish.
To finish in style
To finish in grace
To finish you up,
on your *eternal race,*
this side of heaven.
The one HE's spoken of
through centuries of past.
HE'LL *reed* them a punch,
without giving them lunch.
HE'LL land them on the ground
for HIS assorted finish.

Joshua 1:9, Psalms 68:4

Prophetic Utterances

THE DRONE OF DECEPTION

HE doesn't need any spinach
because HE'S as strong
as can be,
from start to finish.
It's HIS final plan
on the world down below,
in which the enemy
stole *the show,*
and brought torment
down below.

He really *tried* to tie
you up,
from start to finish.
He *tried* to delay you too—
in his own special way,
making you feel late.
It's *not* good for you
his assorted style.
Just remember:
He is *the king of denial,*
trying to break THE CROSS
and make it a loss.

He came to save the lost
right from *his cross*...
and to cause division
at all costs.
Denial, all the while
stooping to lows
no man ought to go.
Rendering them weak
all down below.

The Cry of His Heart

Weakness in numbers
Weakness in ways
Weakness in the way
they behave.

Weakness on trial
Weakness galore
Weakness from mountain
tops
and much, much more.

Too weak to climb
Too weak to crawl
Too weak, too weak
one and all.

He *tries* to render them *weak,*
he's really quite a *chump,*
to render MY chosen ones
without giving a flip!

He'll *pay* for his crimes.
He'll *pay* the price.
He'll *pay* without arms
to point to heaven,
and all around,
while he's on his way down.
It'll *not* be hard to see
as he spirals
down, down and down.

He'll sink to new levels
he's never gone before.
He'll sink and stink
from eternal damnation.

He *won't* get to play
his demonic play station,
his weapon of war.
He'll sink and sink
and sink some more,

Prophetic Utterances

from heavenly places—
to way low places.

Nothing is missed
Nothing is lost.
It's why JESUS chose to die,
to make HIS final cry.
From start to finish,
He'll really diminish
in the world throughout,
not making them
scream and cry
throughout the land—
every girl and boy
every woman and every
man.

He'll pay his price
and it *won't* be very
nice.
It's the reason he gave
you "lice" for trying to be
nice.

He'll *sink* down below
he'll *sink* in his mire
he'll *sink* down below
in his *stink* and his fraud.
He'll *sink* below
and be in a fog.

A *fog* of destruction
A *fog* of denial
A *fog* from heaven
sent down to cover
his pride,
and to expose his nature.

He gave you "lice"
which isn't quite nice.

The Cry of His Heart

To *make* you feel
disgusted and disgraced.

To *make* you be in misery
To *make* you embarrassed
To *make* you feel maimed
To *make* you distracted
from MY HAND which is
upon you.

MY darling little lamb
he sought to destroy you.
He sought to withhold you
from ME.
It's why he fought you
so hard, so you wouldn't
get to ME.
He *devised* little plans
to get you totally off
track
to *make* you a shame
and a total disgrace.

It *was* his style
it *was* his taste
to *make* you
feel like a *total waste*.
A *waste* in the land
A *waste* everywhere
A *wasteland* of eternity
A *wasteland* in society
A *wasteland*, a *wasteland*
forever as such.

His plan went *awry*
his plan did *not* work
his plan met MY demand
on *the eternal crook*.

Prophetic Utterances

He *stole* from your wallet
he *stole* from your purse,
all that he could *steal*
from this universe.

He's really *the curse*
from heaven above.
He curses everyone
every once in a while.
He has no taste
or any style.

He's *the king of misery,*
a worm in the land.
He has been set free
from his rendezvous
of miserable melodies
and such.

He'll go the mile, as
he sails down below.
Not on the shoreline,
but *submerged* down below.
Submerged in his mire
Submerged in his clay
Submerged in his hail,
fire and brimstone
and so much more.

It's his *final day*
It's his *final hour*
to confuse and conflict
with his devilish drip.

He *drips* from the heavens
He *drips* from the skies
He *drips* deceit and lies
He *drips* for fun and
pleasure from underneath.
He *drips* all over you

The Cry of His Heart

and ME.
He *drips* for sheer enjoyment,
to pass the time of day.

He *drips not* for refinement
or any kind of flavor.
He *drips* to keep you
from your SAVIOR
who died on THE CROSS.

He *dries* and he *drips*
without giving a flip!
He is the *royal king of drip*.
He's abandoning his ship
to sail to his harbor.
to dock his ship *"Drip."*
To embark on his journey
to finish his story—
of Jealousy and Torment
and Earthly Wiles.

He has *no* class or
any good style.
He is *the king of denial*.
He was here for a season.
He was here for a while,
but I'M sending *this king*
down awhile,
to reveal his nature
and his crafty denial.

He *thinks* he's funny
he *thinks* he's grand
he *thinks* his jokes
at you are your
final finish.

He doesn't know
how far he'll go below.

Prophetic Utterances

It's impossible to reach,
impossible to know.

He's *weathered* the miles
He's *weathered* the snow
He's *weathered* us out
and it's time for him
to go.

To go to the north shore,
of heaven beneath.
To be pushed and shoved
for his eternal breach
of MY Heavenly Throne.

His *breach* of contract
His *breach* of contempt
His *breach* of glory
to try to rewrite
*The Story of Love
and Grace,*
to line one up from
disgrace to disgrace.

It has been his race
from before you were
born,
to drop you to your
knees and call you
a thorn.

It's the way he plays
the game,
aiming to win it.
This side of heaven
This side of grace,
on all the human race.

Pointing his finger
pointing at THE CROSS
counting it forever lost.

The Cry of His Heart

It's how he spins it
It's how he plays.
To *make* you diminish
before your days
are finished,
to get you out of the
way.

Any way he "spins it"
it's all quite a loss—
He is *the eternal dross
dripping* from his self-made
cross of denial.
His cross of despair
His cross of deception
His cross for all loss.

He is *the king of misery—
this loser of life!*
He has *life eternal*
in eternities finish
of *forever fire,
forever flames.*

It's how he *chose*
to play the game,
from start to finish
to only diminish
THE ONE and ONLY ONE
THE KING OF DAYS.

Not, the king of the night.
His name spells *decay*
across all the land.
His name spells *misery*
throughout his home.

He's really *no king* at all
he's just a *drone*.
A *drone* from society

Prophetic Utterances

A *drone* of misery
A *drone* whose
been knocked off
his deception throne
of *malady* and *misery*
and *disasters* and such.
He makes ME so sick
I want to *upchuck*.

Upchuck his flavor
Upchuck his style
Upchuck his misery
and earthly denial.

He'll go to trial for
his assorted deeds.
He'll take a break
from his earthly
tirades
with his earthly bums.
Who really *aren't*
friends of MINE.
They are really *chums*.

Chums from *the devil*
of earthly denial.
Chums forever in denial.
Chums of dross
Chums of loss
who made a mockery
of MY CROSS.

MY CROSS evens *the score*
of the whole human race.
He deplores it!
He points at it!
It's the disgrace on
his face.

The destruction of him

The Cry of His Heart

this eternal scar—
who *scarred* ME up
for all humanity to see.
He *scarred* ME
He *maimed* ME
While I carried THE CROSS
On *bended* knee
On *bended* brow
On *bended* soil
On *bended* shores
On *bended* rivers
and oceans and streams
galore.

He *wouldn't* bend his knee to ME.
He *wouldn't* even try
he *wouldn't*, he *wouldn't!*
That's why I had to die
to save you and I.
To save you from trouble
and further disgrace.
I'LL *spray* him from
heaven all over his face.
I'LL *confuse* him from heaven
I'LL *confuse* him for awhile
I'LL *confuse* him for a day
and forever all the while.

This king of denial
is about to go to trial
for mistreating MY loved ones
without any style or grace
on his face.
He is a *waste*,
a *doorman of shudder*
an *usher* from down below
on his *unheavenly*
show.
He's about to take *a blow*

Prophetic Utterances

from beginning to finish.
Not sure how he'll finish,
not for him to know.
He'll eat earthly spinach
on this side of heaven.
He'll pay the price
for *not* being so nice.
He'll be put in a vise.
a heavenly container
without any remainder
for anyone to see.
He'll be washed up forever
in *misery*.

Misery takes her captives
and pulls them in the moss
of captivity.
Misery loves company—
it's plain to see.
Misery is in search
of you and of me.

It clasps its hands
at the whole human race
Misery travels *only*
and is *never* free.
Free to love *the lost*,
love the ones
sent by MY FATHER
and HIS ONLY
TRUE SON.

THE FATHER and SON
are about to make
THEIR debut.
THEY'LL introduce themselves
mile by mile,
in THEIR own special style.
Style so rich we can't
add up *the cost*—

The Cry of His Heart

because JESUS went to
THE CROSS.
HIS Story to finish,
to make a way for
the likes of you and me.

To bring forth life
and life indeed,
and set you all free.

Free from *the demon of
death, lies and misery.*
From *this eternal dross*
all that he tried to do
is all his loss
to name a few,
including you and ME
by the shake of his dice,
by the way he led
with *misery*.
His day is done!

His day of *doom* and *dread*
are really quite
close.
Close as the nose
on your face.
It's *his day of tribulation,
his day of disgrace.*
He'll be trodden low.
How low will he go?
It's too far for you to know.

It'll be *The Show* of all shows
from start to finish
on *this earthly worm.*
He'll spin and win it,
for eternity, *lost* and
forsaken.
He's really only bacon,

Prophetic Utterances

this pig of the Nile.
He really had no
business at your trial
for your kids.
He blew a kiss of misery,
aiming at you and ME.

Isaiah 14:9-21; Revelation 3:9, 12:7-11, 20:1-3

The Cry of His Heart

YOU'LL BE FREE

HIS eyes are always
watching you,
no matter how
you spin it.
To make you win it
for now, and all eternity.

It's all not a loss
the time you have left.
HE'LL bless you
no matter how you
spin it.

It's *a royal date*
in store for you.
Blue is befitting you
blue is your style.
Mile for mile
you've run *the race*.
You've finished
your course.

Now, it's time for you
to take your place.
No more disgrace
No more shame
No more denial.

I'VE finished MY Score
I'VE finished MY Race
evening *the score*.
There will be *no more*
sin,
which I deplore.
No more pain and suffering
No more!

Prophetic Utterances

You'll be free to worship ME
in the land of the living,
Not, the land of the dead.

I'LL share your gladness and joy
instead of your misery and toil.
You'll be *free* of the turmoil.
Free of the judges for eternity.
You'll be *free* to worship ME
unhindered, unblocked, unspoken
and untouched.

You'll worship ME with hands
lifted up, all the way up,
without a crutch to hinder you
any longer.
You'll be *free* to worship ME
worship ME indeed.

Sent by MY FATHER
with *LOVE.*
It's what movies are made of:
heavenly movies
heavenly shows
heavenly shouts
in the world throughout
all the land.

It is HIS royal command
it is HIS royal decree
to set you *all free*
from misery.
No more chains to bind you
No more ropes that choke.
Only love—love eternal
forevermore.

So *don't* give up now!
Don't stop getting ready for
This New Day

The Cry of His Heart

It's on its way!
It's not too far off!
You'll see some day.

I'M for you *not* against you.
Not, for a minute would
I let you go.
Not, for a second of time.
You're MINE and MINE alone.
You belong to ME for all
the world to see.

You seek MY glory and
MY face.
You seek love from above.
You seek beauty and splendor.
These are MY footprints
in the sand of your soul.
You seek life, beauty and grace.

You are MINE and MINE alone.
No one else can have you,
you're MINE alone.
I'LL wine and dine you
from floor to floor
from door to door.

The Doorway of Heaven
forever you'll stay
forever you'll be
by MY side, throughout
all history.

Sent from above,
these *storms of life*
won't break you.
They'll remake you
into a better you.
They won't outshine
you.

Prophetic Utterances

They won't divide you.
They'll make you strong,
to carry on and finish
your decree.
Sent from THE FATHER
with *LOVE* for the whole
world.

HE loves us with style
HE loves us with grace
HE loves HIS people
HIS human race.
HE'LL love them now
and forevermore.
HE'S that kind of MAN
that kind of *LOVE*.
Sent from
THE FATHER with *LOVE*
HE loves from the heavenlies.
HE loves from high above
HE *LOVES* you, HE *LOVES* you!
It's what HE does.
Loving HIS children
from heaven above,
holding them with
HIS heavenly glove,
designed to catch you
before you die.

So we can see eye to eye
forever and eternity.
That's what's in store
for you, MY friend,
who laid your life down
for ME to use you to
pen MY Plan.
So it can go forth and
spread *This Gospel of Life,
Gospel of Love* to those

The Cry of His Heart

around you,
to name just a few.

You'll be with ME,
by MY side,
I'LL love you forever.

I'LL love you, not like you
for all time.
You're MINE once and for all
from now and through all
eternity strong.
MY strength knows no
limits, no bounds.
MY strength is eternal
MY friend,
taking you from
strength to strength.

HIS MAJESTY is taking for
HIS own
all HIS children
from the earth below,
to reign with HIM
for eternity
taking you to glory.
It is HIS glory
from story to story
with HIS *Never-Ending
Story of Love*
sent by THE FATHER
with *LOVE*.

LOVE from THE FATHER
of glories and glories,
finishing HIS Story
for all the world to see.

You were in search of ME
now, you have found ME

Prophetic Utterances

in your arms of love
and lace.

You're *not* a disgrace.
You're MY chosen child
of the human race.
You made it first place
in your search for ME.
I heard your cries,
all your sighs
held your tears
of fear and sadness.
I'VE held you very close.
Close to MY heart
never, ever will I
let you go.

Thank you for wanting me.
I've felt like YOUR lost child
bumping and falling into
eternity,
scraping and bruising my soul.
Knocked to my knees,
by the hard knocks of this
world.
Knocked down,
but not knocked out.
It's my eternal plight
to be with you and
dine tonight.

Psalms 136:12, Galatians 5:1

ABOUT AUTHOR:

Gail Hamlin is an author, associate publisher, and editor of over 30 reference books pertaining to Native Americans and United States history (published under Gail Hamlin-Wilson) and she is a poet. She is also a member of Southwest Writers. She is the mother of four children and she lives in New Mexico.

Email: authorgailhamlin@gmail.com
Website: www.gailhamlin.wordpress.com

CPSIA information can be obtained
at www.ICGtesting.com
Printed in the USA
LVOW10s1316210518
577936LV00001B/24/P